A Cock-Eyed Comedy

starring Friar Bugeo Montesino
and other fairies of motley
feather and fortune

JUAN GOYTISOLO

Translated by Peter Bush

City Lights Books
San Francisco

First published in Spain with the title *Carajicomedia* by Editorial Seix Barral, Barcelona, 2000

First published in the United States of America in 2005 by City Lights Books

10 9 8 7 6 5 4 3 2 1

Cover design: Stefan Gutermuth
Text design and composition: Harvest Graphics
Editor: Robert Sharrard

A Cataloging-in-Publication record has been established for this book by the Library of Congress.
   ISBN 0-87286-450-2
   ISBN 978-0-87286-450-4

www.citylights.com

CITY LIGHTS BOOKS are edited by Lawrence Ferlinghetti and Nancy J. Peters and published at the City Lights Bookstor,e, 261 Columbus Avenue, San Francisco, CA 944133

Acknowledgements

Juan Alfredo Bellón
Benito Biancaforte
Luis Carandell
Jaime Gil de Biedma
J. Gónzalez Muela
Pablo Jauralde Pou
Francisco Márquez Villanueva
Teresa de Santos
Severo Sarduy
Ángela Selke
Albert A. Sicroff

not forgetting Abbot Marchena, José María Blanco White and Don Marcelino Menéndez Pelayo

CONTENTS

DRAMATIS PERSONAE

Guzmán de Alfarache: Protagonist of a picaresque novel written in two parts by Mateo Alemán (1599, 1604), set in Spain and Italy. Scenes of low life framed within a moralizing confession include a lengthy interlude in the house of a friendly cleric. Alemán came from a family of Jewish conversos. Twice imprisoned, he finally went to Mexico where he died in 1608.

José María Blanco White: The child of an Irish family living in Seville, he witnessed the last public execution of a witch on the orders of the Inquisition in the late 18th century. He abandoned the Catholic Church and Spain for life as a liberal in England where he edited newspapers and taught at Oxford, and went from Anglicanism to Unitarianism. His autobiographical account of experiences of Jesuitical spiritual exercises and other aspects of contemporary Spain is a rare example of soberly passionate personal narrative in the language. He championed the liberation of Latin American colonies. White wrote in Spanish and English. His English work has been translated and prologued by Juan Goytisolo.

Jaime Gil de Biedma: 20th-century poet from a Barcelona bourgeois background. He lived for many years in the Philippines where he worked for the Tobacco Company: his autobiography which narrates his homosexual experiences in the Philippines and Francoist Spain was published posthumously. He wrote spare, ironic and lyrical verse until he felt he no longer had poetic inspiration, unlike some. He was killed by the one-syllabled virus.

Abbot Marchena: 18th-century radical thinker from Andalusia who read Voltaire and had to take refuge in Gibraltar and then revolutionary France. Robespierre made him a member of the editorial board of *L'Ami du Peuple*. He then joined the Girondins, was arrested, and later imprisoned by the Inquisition. Joseph Bonaparte freed him and gave him a pension to enable him to translate Molière. He died destitute in Madrid.

Marcelino Menéndez y Pelayo: Catholic late 19th-century polymath from Santander. His most famous works include *A History of Spanish Heterodox Thinkers* and *A History of Aesthetic Ideas in Spain*. According to one Spanish encyclopedic authority; he "gave many sterile, undernourished brains a fine source of argument to defend politically controversial subjects."

Juan de Mena: Spanish 15th-century poet from Córdoba who studied in Rome as a result of clerical patronage. He was most famous for his poem, *The Labyrinth of Fortune*. He was possibly dragged to death by a mule in Torrelaguna.

Our Southern/Andalusian Lady of the Molls: Protagonist of *La lozana andaluza,* a novel written by Francisco Delicado in Venice in 1528. Its racy, colloquial language dwells on the joys of female sexuality. The following year, he published a work in Italian on how to defeat syphilis.

Francisco de Quevedo y Villegas: Late 16th-century writer, protégé of the Duke of Osuna. He was the author of picaresque novels, satirical and lyrical poetry, a Knight of the Order of Santiago and a virulently obscene polemicist.

Severo Sarduy: Cuban writer left Cuba in 1960 as a voluntary exile. A member of the Tel Quel group, he worked for many years for Parisian publishers and was responsible for promoting avant-garde Latin American literature. His own poetry and prose exudes baroque extravagance and poetic originality, a world of brothels, *santería*, Buddhism and transvestites. He was killed by the one–syllabled virus in 1993.

Father Trennes: Priest and teacher in a novel by Roger Peyrefitte set in a French Catholic boys' boarding-school where he is over-friendly with the boys and pays the price.

Ramón Valle-Inclán: Late-19th-century Spanish novelist, drama-tist and poet from Galicia and creator of an absurdist "esperpento" vision of the Spanish grotesque. He wrote the first great novel about Latin American dictatorships, *Tirano Banderas*, as well as plays satirizing the Spanish military and portraying a mixture of witch-craft and Catholicism in Galician life.

Vida de don Gregorio Guadaña: Hero of a novel written by Antonio Enríquez Gómez, Spanish 17th-century writer from a Portuguese converso background. The Inquisition's attentions forced him into exile in France. Gregorio narrates how he felt in his mother's belly and parental concerns about his likely gender: his mother reasons a daughter may not "rise up" like a boy but "a sin-gle woman may stir up many men and string them from the horns of the moon."

1 THE POET AND FATHER TRENNES

1

I had just noted in my diary *the morning passed as usual, I was in the office*, a declaration of disenchantment, after another tiring spate of nocturnal cruising Panam's and the Cadiz when Pepe startled me with the news: there's a French gentleman on the line and he's asking after you.

The little red light of danger flashed immediately. Could it be the leaden translator of the Peninsula's hundred best resistance poets who impassively perpetrated his deadly verse on the tablets of print of *Les lettres françaises*?

"Who is that?"

"My real name is of no matter. Call me Father Trennes."

"Like Peyrefitte's character?"

"Just so. The one in *Les amitiés particulières*. A delightful book, don't you agree? But I don't just read novels. I translate Cavafy in my moments of leisure. If you have a minute to spare, I would love to meet you for coffee."

I invited him home the following day, after I'd checked Gabriel and Cuckoo could join me. They were as puzzled as I was. A polyglot priest and translator of Cavafy isn't usually on the menu, at least not in this downtrodden Spain of ours. I had to postpone my visit to a nephew who had succumbed to scarlet fever.

We were expecting, or rather I was, the visitation of a priest soutaned to his ankles, betraying all the attributes and trimmings of office and suitably sanctimonious. Instead, Pepe ushered into the parlor a man in his forties, dressed executively, with a touch of that stuffy stiffness one finds in the stalwart evangelical missionaries who propagate their faith door to door in Oxford. But it was a deceptive first impression soon belied by a telling combination of detail: long, wavy hair, a halo of perfume or aftershave, a designer foulard, svelte Italian shoes and silk socks. A discreet gold crucifix adorned his immaculate shirt-front.

He introduced himself with a display of modesty: though a priest of the Eastern Rite charged by the Pope to take the Virgin of Fatima to Russia, he was a member of the Cosa Santa and usually resided in Parioli. But he enjoyed, he hastened to add, a special dispensation. His linguistic expertise — Classical Greek and Aramaic — had transformed him into a kind of itinerant ambassador for the Apostolic Prelature in the Near East.

"I have come from Rome invited by a team of researchers based at the Cosa's University in Navarra. They have just scientifically proved the truth of the mystery of transubstantiation, the actual presence of Our Lord in a freshly consecrated wafer! A first, placing Spain in pole position among the world's most advanced societies, do you not think?"

Was he serious? Impossible to tell. His face was as guileful as it was deadpan. He digressed endlessly about common friends: Saint Juan of Barbès-Rochechouart, the young Philippine lad working for the Tobacco Company who was apparently his servant. Then he tried to find out if I knew the Seminarist in the pink soutane.

"I don't know whom you can be referring to."

"She insists you met her in a pious little café in the Barrio Chino. You don't remember her? Well, she is a bit of a fantasizer, maybe the encounter is a delusion of hers."

Silence ensued.

"Do you live in the Cosa's Residency?"

"No way! I see to my own needs. I've rented a humble flat in San Gervasio. I'll move in on my return from the University of Navarre."

(When I later visited him, he showed me into a sitting room of an unmistakably sixties bourgeois vintage: green-upholstered three-piece suite, marble side-table littered in medical advice journals, grey moquette and a four-pronged chandelier. Everything exuded conventionality and inane wealth: well-stocked larder and wardrobe, austerely elegant images and crucifixes and the devoted attentions of blessed cleaning ladies or assistant numeraries, as the Father called them. Nevertheless, next to the Kempis of our era, on his office table the statuette of a Greek ephebe stood erect.)

Gabriel, Cuckoo and I were highly intrigued, pricked by a rather perverse curiosity towards this chap's ways and by-ways. Was he? Of course he was or, as I recalled quoting Lorca, he was wasting his time. His suave manner and religious unction married with the titters and fleeting frisson of guilt of someone afraid to show his hand and keen to exercise reserve. Cavafy and the Hellenic adolescents seemed more a false trail than a confession. "He declared his telegram-boys but kept quiet about the postmen!"

I invited him to join us another afternoon for drinks with my publisher and his Icelandic friend. As if scenting danger, he alleged an unavoidable appointment with someone close to the Monsignor, then finally acquiesced.

"Chartreuse, Bénédictine?"

"My aunts, may they rest in peace, would call that a tot. I'm not sure if it was a liqueur or anis."

"Take your pick from the bottles in the cabinet. Pepe, serve the gentleman."

After a brief cutchikoo, Father Trennes opted for a gin and tonic.

"Careful, don't overdo the gin or it will make me tipsy," he warned.

Precisely what I was hoping for, to get him tipsy, as he put it, and go on a fling accompanied by his holiness to the bars on the Rambla and Escudillers. My publisher ensured his glass was never empty and with peasant cunning, we egged him on.

"Were the rumor-mongers right about the Father's life and miracles: about his charismatic appearances in a black Cadillac and *nouveau riche* fondness for giving audiences in silk-lined rooms with enameled chests, glass cabinets with Chinese ivory marquetry, bronze lamps and clocks, Coromandel screens and coats of arms? Indeed, was it a fact that a genuflecting maiden placed a silver tray of correspondence on the table where Monsignor breakfasted as frugally as ever?"

"Aghh!," responded Father Trennes. "A load of envious tittle-tattle! Fishwives on a roll! The Father's precepts of simplicity and humility give the lie to such malign slanders."

But the gin and tonics took their toll and, by the time Cuckoo and Pigtail arrived, Father Trennes agreed to partner them in a *paso doble*. It was the one I'd heard as a child in the fiestas in La Nava. I would sometimes have it on in the background, as a counterpoint to my translation of Eliot or, when accompanied by some pretty boy, on the jukebox in Panam's. A fifth or sixth sense (inevitably the sixth!) suggested it would be a night to remember and it was. A sudden excitement had gripped everyone, as if each of us had assumed the deep truth of these lines by Verlaine:

N'as-tu pas fouillant en les recoins de ton âme
Un beau vice à titer comme un sabre au soleil?

I deliberately turned up the volume (my parents were out of town and Pepe had beat a tactful retreat). The rhythm of the *paso doble* gradually raised the emotional pitch: our respectable family parlor seemed more like a ring at the fair or a bull-run. Pigtail brandished with brio the foulard of Cuckoo who'd purloined a pair of fans from the glass cabinet, and was whirling them like *banderillas*. Then, Father Trennes turned Miura bull. A red quilt! I fetched a faded pink specimen which I handed to Pigtail. The good priest pawed the parquet with his elegant hoofs before making for the cloth. Cuckoo goaded him roaring like a lioness on heat. Our pedigree youngster wasn't afraid of ridicule. Flustered and rather unbuttoned, he performed to script with the fury of the possessed. The *paso doble* turned us on: its crescendo *bien arrosé* with gin was a perfect arouser. After a few minutes we felt exhausted. Father Trennes wrapped the pink quilt round his shoulders and asked: "How'd I be as a flamenco dancer?" "Like a mad cow, honey!" cried Cuckoo. He tried a few steps, but couldn't. The regular offerings of gin and tonic had done the trick. He was drunk and started singing.

(It was one of the ditties his "colleagues" used to sing in the sense that term carries, according to Juan G., in the Moroccan dialect of Arabic.)

He couldn't resist being bundled into our cortège of two taxis to the shifting sands of Panam's. There we poured him two more rounds of his favorite tipple and I introduced him to a well-dressed hunk with the demeanor of a public schoolboy. But my brokering failed. Father Trennes showed not a flicker of interest in the youth. Perhaps he preferred adolescents like the poet he translated or mustachioed beefcake with the looks of a security guard. That dive contrived items of neither variety. The mystery persisted although, as Gabriel said subsequently, "You can bet while he's closing his hands in prayers, he's opening up something else!"

What happened afterwards in the early hours I could only recall later from the depths of my hangover. I took the spurned youth (a good professional, but no real conviction) to the Hotel Cosmos and my publisher and his friend escorted Father Trennes to the flat in San Gervasio. They had to help him out of the taxi: he'd got hiccups and was sobbing hysterically: That is quite finished! Never more! *Mon Dieu, quelle déchéance!* They had to open the door for him (apparently he couldn't hit the keyhole), dissolve two Alka-Seltzers in a glass of water and settle him into bed.

As I penned these lines, I remembered a few lines by Cavafy, probably translated by our Father:

And how dreadful the day when you give in
(the day you let yourself go, and you give in).

2

For a number of years I lost sight of good Father Trennes.

I discovered he'd gone to Cuba to salute Fidel Castro's Revolution. By all accounts he sang the praises of its portents and marvels. Perhaps he liked mulattos? Wagging tongues reckoned he did: "Like the real saint he is, he goes after the all-healing whey of the Lucumi. *On l'appelle déjà l'Abbesse de Castro!*"

Back in Europe, he set up in Paris. I'd already sent him the address on the rue Poissonnière and supposed he was in contact with Juan though neither made mention of it. The almost painful, wholehearted energy I seek in bed no longer galvanized me as before. Was I getting old? Yes, I probably was.

Fortunately, greater mental strength and also greater calm and confidence accompany that process. Marguerite Yourcenar, whose work I plunged into after shelving la Beauvoir, expresses it very well in a quotation, taken like the Verlaine, from Robert Liddell's excellent biography of Cavafy which the Father lent me:

L'angoisse, en matière sensuelle, est presque toujours un phenomène de jeunesse; ou elle détruit un être, ou elle diminue progressivement du fait de l'expérience, d'une plus juste connaissance du monde, et plus simplement de l'habitude.

But to return to Father Trennes. He occasionally phoned me at the office: "Oh, I can see you so happy breathing in the air of the Ramblas! *Ici, il pleut dans la ville, et il pleut dans mon coeur, comme dit Brassens.* Send me a little ray of sunshine: a poem, a letter, a photo of you with a pretty boy!" After his rash of Castroism subsided, he prudently steered away from politics and revolutionary ideals. Nor did he tramp the calle de Vitrubio, or, very exceptionally, the Via Bruno Buozzi. According to Juan, he lived a life dedicated to his apostolic endeavors in places of very dubious sanctity.

One day he turned up at my flat in Turó Park: untouched by

the passage of time, long-haired and dressed with an elegant insouciance, very sixty-eightish. (A few weeks before he'd called me excitedly from Cairo: he'd just opened his heart to a traffic cop in the busiest square in the city! What had been his response? "Oh he was perfect! He went on with his whistle but agreed to meet me in front of the Egyptian Museum." He sighed: so tall and strong, his feet like a grape picker's out of Velázquez.)

"You look as fresh as a daisy! Are you on a course of hormones in the fatherland of Ceaucescu?"

"I don't need to go to Romania like some television announcer. I try to live a healthy life while waiting for my next reincarnation."

He'd finally found his sense of humor. He told me about his new friends in Paris: Severo Sarduy, Roland Barthes, François Wahl. What about Genet? He worshipped him from afar but was intimidated by his rude ways. As for his relationship with the rue Poissonnière he suffered from Juan's topsy-turvy moods, "ever more engrossed in himself and his labyrinthine writing."

He was apparently preparing—or perpetrating—a novel that the author himself dubbed a door-stopper, tome or artifact—whose production required extensive reading and years of labor. A history of sexuality in the light of Catholic doctrine via a journey through the Spanish language from the Middle Ages to the present. He wanted to transcribe his cruising experiences in church language, including that of the author of the contemporary Kempis, in order to parody it from within and strip bare its hypocrisy: what, perhaps contaminated by his *Tel Quel* readings, he called "textual libido." We both laughed.

"Is it an autobiography or a novel? Does it have plot, chapters, real people?"

Plot is the least of his worries, Father Trennes argued at second remove. Our mutual friend is trying to train his ear to catch the voices from the past in order to appropriate them and become lord and master of his writing, forgetting those striving to do just that in relation to literature and the literary life. One could thus measure an artist's vitality by his ability to assimilate the different literary tendencies of the tradition in which he inscribes himself at the behest of a vast, ambitious and original project (didn't Eliot write something similar?). Whoever tried to bypass this substratum or digested library, *jamais en rapport avec les combinaisons mercantiles* (to quote Mallarmé), was condemned to live and disappear with his era . . . Father Trennes doubted the viability of such a project and so did I. Forced to choose between Forster and Bakhtin, I always stick with Forster's reasonable precepts and parameters. But I awaited an opportunity to argue the toss with Juan.

"Et vous, mon père" (I always address him as *vous* in order to mortify him), "how's life treating you round Barbès and the Gare du Nord?"

"I'm no longer Father Trennes!"

I'd served him gin on the rocks which he savored with relish.

"I've changed my *nom de guerre*, like the whores of yesteryear! Now I'm Friar Bugeo. Doesn't the name ring any bells?"

It did in fact, but I couldn't hit on which.

"He wrote *A Cock-eyed Comedy*, a work of saintly shamelessness, a short, sharp exchange included in the *Book of Burlesque Songs*. Aren't you familiar with it?"

The anachronisms of ex-Father Trennes and greenhorn Friar Bugeo delighted me. Had he, as I'd urged Juan, hitched up to the English literary tradition from Sterne to Swift? I remember we bantered about his longevity. A century and a half? From the Early Middle Ages! We lingered on Jehovah's fantastic computations and the earthly affections of the patriarchs in *Genesis*. But could one doubt the word of God? He quoted lines of Milton at me; I riposted with a reflection from Gracián. It ended in stalemate.

He poured himself another gin with lots of ice.

"Let's go straight to the point," he said quite seriously. "Do you not believe in transmigration?"

Years later, when I was recovering from the ritual, exhausting journey to the Antipodes (the *Filipinos* bored me, no longer aroused me), I received by registered post the manuscript into which, cruel reader, you will now sink your teeth: tear it up if you feel that way. I don't mind and it doesn't reflect on me. I passed it on to the publisher just as it came. If there's anything to criticize, it's Peeping Tommery. I wrote a poem on this practice in my youth. I was a poet once and, when the word left me, I left that blessed state.

2 MANUSCRIPT I: MY SAINTS AND THEIR WORKS

A PROLOGUE FOR INSIDERS

A Cock-Eyed Comedy, that gracious arbor of exemplary lives and deeds by Friar Bugeo Montesino, was published for the first time in the 1519 Valencia edition of the *Book of Burlesque Songs*. The anonymous prologuer tells how when leafing one day through the pious author's sermons and epistles he found "the work that this reverend Father composed for his recreation" and, because it was "a devout, contemplative thing," he decided to bring it into the light of day. Probably written in the brief reign of Philip the First the Beautiful and Joanna the Mad, the text sheds no light on its enigmatic creator, "a priest or friar, perhaps even a Trinitarian."

Friar Bugeo Montesino's personality remains swathed in a mist of countless legends and fables. Although some scholars set the date of his death at the beginning of the reign of Emperor Charles the First, others argue that, disguised as a Greek Archimandrite, he tried to help Saint John of the Cross in the Toledan dungeon where he was rotting, a victim of the rage and envy of the Carmelite Order, and that he was even present, with his loyal flunky, at a sinister interdisciplinary colloquium on mysticism and the Saint's poetry in a crepuscular spa on the shores of the Black Sea.

Be that as it may, he didn't abandon his apostolic mission, and re-emerged in the 1960s as a Cosa Santa activist, without renouncing his position in the ecclesiastical hierarchy in the Churches of the Eastern Rite or the Papal commission to transport the image of the Virgin of Fatima to Russia and oversee its conversion to our Credo. First in Barcelona, then in Paris and different missionary territories, he preached by word and deed the way to holiness and mingled with writers of the caliber of Genet, Barthes, Sarduy, Jaime Gil de Biedma and Juan Goytisolo, whom he occasionally alludes to as "the copyist" and his "disciple in Barcelona," making fun of his literary poaching and undue appropriation of the diaries, drafts and notes in the First Part of his work in order to concoct fictitious novels and autobiographies of his own.

At the end of "The Hidden Dwellings"—the second part of the new, tasty version of *A Cock-Eyed Comedy* that we will offer the reader *tout de suite*—Friar Bugeo Montesino states he withdrew from the world after bequeathing his pious manuscripts to the Fondazione Vaticana Latinitas. In keeping with such declarations, he took shelter like the hermits of old in the fastnesses of Mauritania Tingitana, accompanied by several saints of rugged, well-honed virtue, with whom he recites canonical prayers and surrenders himself to many a fervorous spiritual exercise aimed at edifying the youngsters and guiding them along the Broad Paths of grace and consolation.

Lakdar

He appeared before my eyes, a sudden theophany, on the boulevard Rochechouart: he was sitting on a bench opposite the Elysée

Montmartre, where I used to repair with friends to the Sunday wrestling contests, sometimes with Jean Genet. He was back from his usual survey of the chapels to which I was predisposed—the Emperor Vespasian cottages scattered between Stalingrad and Pigalle—and, if you'll excuse the daring allusion, I was stunned like Saul on the road to Tarsus.

Lakdar was a swarthy lad with a handlebar mustache, hard features and jet-black eyes which seemed to harbor, in the words of my distinguished copyist, "a tiger's implacable stare." He was chatting to friends and I waited patiently for him to bid farewell to them before I went over and suggested a meditative exercise in the nearby Square d'Anvers. I revealed my devotion straight away—less afraid of an uncouth reaction than a polite no—but he accepted immediately and flustered me mightily. *Je suis sans sou*, he told me. We went to one of my intimate refuges and I enjoyed the glories of that body that was to be the object over the years, despite life's vicissitudes and hard knocks, of a pristine cult of dulia: unnerving visions of his erect member, facial hieratism, big, rough hands, an innocent brutality. His steely gaze on the ascent to the summit betrayed no sentiment: only brilliance, wildness, inscrutablity. I helped him with largesse and we set a rendezvous for the following day in the Square so we might join in new prayers.

Lakdar had enlisted in the French army during the war with Algeria. Despite being a *harki* he'd not resolved in time his status as a national and found himself a candidate for deportation after conviction for petty theft. He had no legal aid and didn't seem to realize the period for appeal had elapsed. As if anticipating the precarious nature of our Parisian devotions, I took him to get a passport photo in the Luxor Cinema in Barbès.

I tried to find him a lawyer but the courts beat me to it. One afternoon, after hurrying to a café where we'd agreed to meet, a friend of his—a baker who exhibited his hefty baguette in the boulevard chapels from dusk to dawn—informed me he'd been arrested in a police raid and transferred to the detention center in the Cité. I tried to get a stay of sentence but failed. All I achieved was to entrust the duty-policeman with a bag with a change of clothing and a letter addressed to the Cosa.

The reply, obviously dictated in rural Arabic and translated into baroque French by a public scribe, evoked "exquisite moments of unheard-of pleasure," unfurled a garland of flowery declarations of love and concluded in a surprising envoi—given it was to me— "I kiss your beautiful black eyes."

(Over half a rosary of years, I received numerous variations on this epistolary theme. Often identical, the formulas seemed copied from a popular manual for composing letters of love and friendship.

When I was sent to New York to preach by example, I was visited by a North American colleague I'd got to know through mutual friends. His saint—a Tetuan who feigned a great passion for him and introduced him to a supposed sister, in fact an attractive girl on the game, in order to get her into the villa they both shared and bed her on the side—wrote him letters in phonetic Spanish which I lovingly translated. I can remember his deep sighs as I translated into English "you love of my life" and other such phrases. The missives always ended with harrowing pleas for help. The North American would ask me: "Do you think he loves me as strongly as he affirms?" I sidestepped that one as best I could or piously deceived him: I thought it cruel to disenchant him of a love so ardent. On one occasion he asked for a thousand dollars for a visa and the Tangier–New York airfare. I knew he was lying—a visa was not available to a man without a trade whose only income was the giros from his "love"—and, weeks later, the heartbroken lover came to the Mission's headquarters: the Tetuan had reneged on his promises to travel, had suffered various disasters and demanded yet more cash. He left me sobbing and I heard no more of him until years later: he was pushing up daisies in a cemetery after the eruption and calvary of the one-syllabled monster. May God take pity on his soul!)

As soon as I could I flew from Alicante to Oran. Lakdar was waiting for me at the airport: he wore an old djellaba and the palms of his hands were dyed with henna. I brought him a good supply of clothing: shirts, trousers, jackets, even one of those ties he liked to flaunt in all his personal, unruly elegance. We went to the Hotel Royal but they wouldn't put him on the list of residents: the authorities denied him a national I.D. card because he'd been a *harki* in the pay of the French. The only solution, agreed with the receptionist in exchange for a tip, was to allow him to come up to my room for a quick prayer before breakfast. Although anxiety and furtive liaisons have their attractions, I soon tired of the routine: I searched out and found a one-story house, unmistakably Spanish in style, down-at-heel but with a large bed. I spent several days there with the future Tarik of the novel by my dedicated, wise copyist, transfigured by much mutual devotion, by the glowing incandescence of our credos and ejaculatories. I've often lamented my total lack of talent as a painter and drawer: impossible to bring to card or canvas the tens, the hundreds of sketches inspired by his leathery, robust form. Lakdar polished and purified the pugnacious vein of his works until he was transformed into the instrument, firm as a steel spigot, of the holiness preached by our Founder.

I rented a Renault 4 to drive to his birthplace. His uncle lived there, a National Liberation Army veteran, and timely or untimely director of a "socialist farm" expropriated from some settler. He welcomed us warmly and invited us to a couscous with the other men in the family. He implied that his nephew had no future in Algeria: as his mother was from Oujda, why didn't he seek his fortune in Morocco?

In 1968 — I can't pinpoint the exact date — the letter dictated by Lakdar carried a stamp with the face of Hassan II. As I read I understood the Moroccan consulate had given him a pass and he'd crossed the frontier to reach his mother's family's village. I hurried to catch the plane to Oujda, met Lakdar in the airport and hired a taxi to go to his home. I spent the night there, in a tiny bedroom, while he did his duty by a shy, reserved girl: his silent wife. I remember how the whole family congregated around me when I shaved with the help of a bowl of water and pocket mirror. My curiosity regarding the new bride and the circumstances of the wedding remained unsatisfied. Nobody in the village spoke French beyond the usual polite formulas.

We returned to Oujda intending to spend a few days there but the police registered the presence of Lakdar in the hotel reception and took him to the police station to question him on the outward signs of his secret graces. He denied the sanctity of his works and was released. The following day, troubled by the administrative restraints on my missionary labors, we travelled to Tangier. The Cosa headquarters welcomed a new guest: there followed another brief but intense period of beatific bliss.

We meandered through the city where my insatiable data-collector sites his putative novel, mapped possible itineraries, noted down names of squares and alleyways. My old acquaintances—whether colleagues or not—seemed intimidated by the presence of that brawny, mustachioed fellow with the looks of a gendarme or sergeant-major. My bodyguard, a man of few words, preached by deed and example and, after the *de rigueur* prayers, to show his readiness for fresh, improving exercises, he kept his standard flying high. Several snapshots show him in the streets or restaurants we favored: dark, strong, handsome, his nocturnal eyes smoldering like embers.

We twice repeated the *sursum corda* in the Tangier oratory. Between sermons and homilies I bought him clothes and shoes for his numerous family, which I tried to maintain as best I could. I kept sending giros to his village, as I did with Mohammed, until the will of the Lord led me to fresh, absorbing pastures. Stricken with remorse, I stopped answering his letters—but, how could I possibly sustain the great number of souls on fire who longed to be assuaged?

Abdullah

When the Lord crossed our paths, he had been resident for years in France. He'd lived in Grenoble and sustained saintly intercourse with a cinema-owner. He sometimes mentioned him and his daughter, the solicitous father offered her to him as a virgin, allegedly, for him "to stretch her": typical braggadocio on his part concerning the virtues of his infallible instrument. As I noted at the onset, he was very devious: he liked to horse-trade but, faced by my determination, he finally opted for a more enduringly correct attitude. Our joint, usually improvised, prayer meetings thus continued for more than fifteen years.

I found him one night in the oratory by the now defunct cinema, the Palais de Rochechouart. He was displaying the strength and size of his pestle in the center stall of that shrine and, impressed by the vigor of his argument, I invited him to emerge and strike a deal. I proposed *imo pectore* a shared meditation but he feigned a novice's scruples, pretended not to understand my project, asked for advance payment until I got tired and desisted. Days later, it was he who rushed to greet me: we propped up the bar of a café tabac of Tote addicts and, through the veil of his come-on trousers, he alerted me to the readiness of his hard-on. In the give and take—while he took advantage of the crush to rub my meat—we agreed to put his mettle to the test at evensong.

Abdullah is a blue-eyed Berber—I think the only one on the long list of those I've helped during my apostolacy—leathery-faced, a lean, muscular body endowed by God in His infinite goodness with a sagrarium the bulk, length and thickness of which I've calibrated but four or five times in my righteous life.

(It came to mind the day M.P., a cheerful, carefree, adulterous parishioner, recounted to me within the secret bower of the confessional, her singular charismatic initiation: the deflowerer, a Buenos Aires doctor, had been favored by nature with an enormous phallus. "Now I've seen hundreds of every size possible, I swear his was the biggest yet." Once over her swooning, she tried someone else: "*Son zizi* was the smallest ever." Her heroic efforts had met on fields of feather. But then, tormented by the disparity between her only points of reference, she exclaimed, "I went mad, tossed and turned every night in bed worrying, my God, where lies the truth?")

Stark, with a frothy head and juicy monstrance, Abdullah relished the splendor of his scepter, skilfully held court, kissed with that conviction that is the gift, according to my friend Genet, of North African saints. He also took my hope and glory in hand, revived it, loved to discover its secret laws. Everything had a price and, boy, did he bargain: he combined his beady, begging arts with a playful toss of his finest hour, the confident pressure of his mustache and hands, the eager attack of his voracious lips, fresh as an open wound. Piety and cunning combined with the vast arsenal of weapons he possessed. His resilient virtue never wavered, never fell by the wayside.

Although we sometimes met on Sundays and public holidays and he was sure of his reward for nailing me, oh so sweet, so rough!; I refused to be moored and roped to his *bite* or bollard. I usually bumped into him when visiting the chapels on the boulevard de Rochechouart or the Gare du Nord's votive shrine where he'd been brandishing his whipper-snapper to the delight of the Sisters of Perpetual Succor: seeing me, he'd stuff it in his fly, clumsily, ingenuously trying to hide his saintly piece. We'd go to one of the accommodating hotels in the 18th *arrondissement* and, if I then stayed on in those climes to read or make notes in my breviary, I'd see him again in the vicinity of some shrine, preparing to alleviate the sufferings of some needy soul.

On one occasion I fetched him by car from the building workers' hostel where he lived and, on the way to the city, he made me stop in wasteland, kneel in the dark and venerate his apostle's staff, like the brothers of Nocturnal Adoration.

Our pious relationship, upon which I entreat hard-pressed souls toiling after salvation to meditate, survived despite numerous long parentheses: my missions to the Maghreb and North America, where more than once I received a letter with a rough sketch of his monument and the geyser spurting from his well: other individual devotions of mine to various saints to which I shall later refer in other chapters of these exemplary lives. But, after a time, we'd meet up and the fervor held. He sometimes escorted me to the Moorish baths on the boulevard Voltaire and, after hallowing me, he'd stay on, insatiably ardent, searching for new hallelujahs steeped in indulgences.

At the beginning of the eighties he became bound by the norms of his pious sect: I once met him by chance and he said he couldn't accompany me because of Ramadan. He'd gone on holiday to Algeria and married a third time (he was widowed by his second wife). We still saw each other in my favorite sanctuaries. He performed with the mastery cognate with prolonged, bodily knowledge: he never failed to splice his sail, never disappointed my desires. The eruption of the one-syllabled monster forced me to change lifestyle and, though he'd stir his steeple in café lavatories, I preferred, with the caution the Lord urges on his souls, not to risk a litany *a cappella* with a saint so prodigious in good works as he. When he returned to his country, he sent me a letter asking me to find work and a bride for his son. But I received no response from him, years later, on the eve of a pastoral visit to Algeria.

As Arab authors in the contemplative vein of Nefzaui say, May God keep his fortress impregnable and may it make his wife happy!

Zinedine

Our paths crossed by chance one afternoon on the boulevard Rochechouart and we both slowed to a halt and greeted each other. He was wearing a dark blue cap that hid his baldness and sported a thick mustache and well-kept beard which his chin nourished, as if compensating for the shiny pate on his powerful, brawny skull.

Born in Oran—seedbed of believers famous for their rigor and endurance—he'd resided in the metropolis from childhood and lived in harness—here today, gone tomorrow—with a Breton woman he did finally marry. Affable and dependable, I never saw him lose his temper or cool. His fondness for the bottle sometimes dragged him downhill: one afternoon I spotted him zigzagging along my boulevard of delights and I dragged him into a hotel where, avoiding the usual homilies, I officiated as guardian angel and fed him coffee and aspirins. May '68 was in full swing and he expressed his contempt for the demonstrators who were insulting the General: *des gonzesses*, he said, *des pauvres cons*! Over time, thanks be to God!, he gave up alcohol.

His lively features, smooth skull, black beard and mustache created a refined but tough profile that contrasted with his urbane ways. For a time he dropped his girlfriend and set up in an attic room in the Porte de Clignancourt area. Its tiny window could be seen from the square, indeed from the exit to the metro, and the days we had a date he'd hang some garment there to confirm he was in port and ready for a broadside. Even so, I once climbed to the top of the stairs and found him at prayer with a Frenchman. He proposed a Trisagion and, in view of my refusal, he sent him packing and I stayed on. Responsible for the management of the building—*el desdichado* had gone to collect the rent and had been unable to resist the temptation to stroke his bulging crotch.

Zinedine possessed a veteran member—a lethal jack-in-the-box—which he affectionately dubbed his "devil." The temper and firmness of its virtue made him one of the most meritorious keepers of the Order of Perpetual Succor.

He would alleviate me twice or thrice and then remain stretched out, an arm around my shoulders, in fruitful, silent contemplation. He said little about his life in Algeria and observed great discretion in relation to mine (I'd never been one to air my selfless labors in bringing relief to the sufferings of bodies and souls). He accepted my donations quite naturally, as a friendly gesture from someone with more possibilities than himself. I don't remember his trade or, rather trades, for he often rang the changes. This period of ardent intimacy, with no restrictions on either side, ended as a result of my long absences, when I embarked on evangelical missions to California, Boston and New York. Back in Paris, after one such, I took the metro to Porte de Clignancourt and walked to his place. But his name had been erased from the list of tenants and the concierge didn't know where he'd gone.

We met again by chance and he accompanied me to the hotel on the rue Ramey which I'd favored over many years because of its owner's warm involvement: I caught him more than once having a peep, his eye stuck to the keyhole of my bedroom door. Zinedine was back with his companion and planned to settle down with her somewhere in Brittany. The last date I had with him ended abruptly. His fellow countryman Kittir, of whom I'd seen neither hide nor hair for some time, lay in wait for me by the royal battleground of my hotel and blocked our way. I had to pursue him in order to avoid a punch-up and jilted my old companion-in-arms (may the Lord forgive this deviation and many others!).

(Months later I received a postcard from Brest. Zinedine had married and seemed happy. As the missive bore no address on the back, I couldn't answer. I harbor hopes that God gives him a long life and peaceful old age: he is one of the best, most conscientious saints I preached to in those years.)

Kittir
The only photo I have of him doesn't really capture his robust, rather truculent mien.

Married and father to numerous offspring, he had the looks of a fairground gypsy or owner of a clay pigeon shoot. He was expansive and inclined to exaggerate although, as I later discovered, his devotion to my person was real enough and was accompanied by feelings of jealousy that fortunately none of my missionary colleagues has ever shown.

(The gamut of emotions within my charitable apostolacy has included trust and friendship, the pragmatism inherent in a mere exchange of services, cases of ephemeral, lucid submission but never the love I reserve for God and His Divine Intercessor.)

We were both meandering by a public shrine that gets very busy at night, beneath the overland metro station of Barbès-Rochechouart, and he followed me near the Square d'Anvers. There he beat the meat, and back in the street, we had a drink in a café now gone, where I'd met Mohammed.

(All the monuments or landmarks in my contemplative life have faded like dreams or were suppressed by cruel bureaucratic decisions taken during the legislature of Valéry Giscard d'Estaing—may he be cursed a thousand times!)

Kittir dragged me unexpectedly, almost forced me into basement lavatories and submitted me to a rough and ready communion with the holy severity and shamelessness encouraged by our Founder. Perhaps because of *in vino veritas*—he was rather far gone—he gave me the address of his building site on the outer boulevards of the Left Bank. I rushed to see him with the alacrity the case called for: he wore the regulation site helmet and a whitewash-stained overall. After his initial surprise and our mutual delight, he invited me to drink tea in his hut and introduced me, to his friends who also lived there, as godfather to one of his children.

From then on we met regularly: we had Sunday lunch in a restaurant that's also no more, where the boulevard Rochechouart meets the rue Clignancourt. During one of those feasts of couscous and vin rosé from Provence, he told his younger brother—a handsome man settled in France with his wife and children—that I was his "soul mate" with whom he shared "bed and board." His brother didn't seem to flinch, even when Kittir, flushed with wine, invited me to visit their village, stay in his house and sleep with him in his bed, "it's all right, we must make sure we don't leave any stains," exuberant, full of himself, mixing wheat with chaff, as he boasted of his dubious adventures with French women subjugated by his virility.

Months later—I'll mention no dates because these blur and fade from the watch-tower of time—I popped in to see him in the workers' hostel where he later lodged. He bantered about how the Algerian in the neighboring bunk often caught him erect and wrapped himself in a precautionary blanket, afraid he'd be violated in his sleep. When he had an accident at work (or was it an operation?), I went to see him in the hospital on the rue Vaugirard. He had a room of his own and my suddent apparition, he later confided, won his heart. With his customary gift of the gab, he related how the nurse, when washing him, had admired the grandeur of his attributes: *votre femme doit être très heureuse avec vous, Monsieur!*

Whether it was truth or flannel—more plausibly the latter—he incited me to put my hand between the sheets where he placed it on his epicenter: the uprising was genuine and glorious!

Nevertheless, his maudlin, possessive ways made me uneasy: my teachings reached out to all souls and privileged none. That's why I didn't see him for several Sundays until the afternoon he caught me with Zinedine at the entrance to the shrine where we labored. He pulled me into a nearby café and tearfully demanded I return the photos he'd given me. He escorted me to the Cosa's local headquarters and waited in the street while I looked for his now useless mementos. He then insisted on sanctifying the evening with a round of prayers. Our impetuous votive candles melted and transmuted into puddles of wax.

We saw each other in our old lair until these encounters declined and my apostolic zeal grew fertile and extended in search of new prodigies and saints.

He returned to his country at the beginning of the seventies and sent me his address. I had planned a visit *ad perpetuam rei memoriam* from Morocco but, after the Green March, the frontier between the two countries became an obstacle. I relented in my attempts and focused the center of my activities in the Medina of so many souls in need of help and succor. I've had no news of him since then. May God preserve his life and fan the flame of his desires!

Abdelkadir

One cold, listless afternoon, as intermittent snow storms quickly melted in the mud and tar of the boulevard Rochechouart, I took refuge in the entrance to the Cinema Trianon, a meeting point for numerous North African immigrants, opposite the tabernacles I favored for my devotions and rapture. Among the half dozen Maghrebis scrutinizing the photo-trailers in the hallway, I registered the presence of one corpulent, scowling fellow, who lingered in contemplation of the half-deserted boulevard and then scurried to the chapel of my delights and disappeared therein. I imitated him right away and occupied the empty stall, adjacent to the center of the Vespasian cottage, in order to spy comfortably on the leisurely flapping of a tool whose solidity and volume had no need to envy Abdullah's. He pursued his exemplary manipulation, absorbed and impassive like a Yucatan idol and not a single facial muscle flinched when I advanced my incredulous hand to his *sancta sanctorum* in order, like Thomas the Apostle, to check out the palpability of his miracle. I said, "Come to the hotel with me." Without saying a word, he buttoned his fly and followed me.

Abdelkadir was in his thirties at the time and worked for the French railways. He'd lost two fingers of his left hand in a work accident and the stumps, like stunted sprigs, added a touch of tempting rough to his figure as a tough, hardbitten worker. For a reason beyond me, our first encounter represented an exceptional engagement: he refused union and time and again offered his magnificence to my hallowed lips. He also turned down my tithe and only took it after I'd insisted.

As our bond lasted a good few years, despite involuntary breaks and missionary interruptions, I could observe with delectation his gradual, much-merited ascension to the higher plane of sanctity. After visiting his family (I think he had a wife and children, but he never mentioned them), he was granted early retirement and compensation for partial incapacity and dedicated his life to contemplative meditation in public urinals until he pulled off a doctorate *honoris causa* in the Gare du Nord. Abdelkadir was a first-rate mace-bearer, his competence and virtuosity mounted from year to year. His wisdom was veritably Thomist in its knowledge of the body's hidden laws: its torments and joys, abysses and climaxes.

He lived by daily parading his timber to win new recruits: it was his work tool, power switch, generator and provider of pleasure and energy. His virtue prospered along broad, tranquil paths; I never saw him exhausted or downcast: if he interrupted the journey, he did so at the request of the one shafted, a happy imitator of Christ on the Cross. Sometimes, he shacked up temporarily with an unsuspecting soul: first, with a Martinican whom I knew by sight, a devout busy bee from the catacombs of the Luxor Cinema, and he profited from his absence from the flat to get super horny in the marriage bed with pink cushions, dolls and accessories bearing an indelible Pronuptia stamp; later with a young teacher of French, about whom more anon.

He usually saw the night out *in oratione* in hotels around Pigalle, Anvers and the Sacré Coeur, where I'd slip in when the concierge nodded off. The thickness of his stump seemed beyond the load capacity of the busiest tunnels and arches. But patient priming and proper lubrication worked miracles. Abdelkadir's clustered fingers learned to play in sensitive, erectile areas, combining imperious strength with gentle kneading.

I followed him on his move to the rue Marx Dormoy: to the poky room in an Algerians' hotel and another by the eponymous metro station, to which room one had access via a backstairs, thus avoiding the noisy crowd packed in the bar. Our invariably chance encounters ended in that monkish cell without running water where he welcomed his devotees. Although I discovered that he had punished avarice by coming to blows with an oblate in Madeleine's knocking-shop—once I tried to take him there to pray a few psalms, but Madame threw his bad behavior in his face and refused him entry to Eden—the fact is he always behaved well towards me. He told me I was one of his three or four most favorite companions in prayer and his complicity as a comrade-in-arms induces me to think it was indeed so. Despite his professionalism and fondness for geometrically varied experiences, our love shared the mysteries of pain and pleasure over many a long year.

His services as consoler of those afflicted by diverse tribulations refined his natural gifts as a stud and widened (praised be the Lord!) the ambit of his charitable works. One day, after a coupling on his bunk, he toasted me with the bitter heat of his hosepipe. On another, when he caught me in the preliminary stages of proselytizing a parishioner of mine—a *harki* who spoke both French and Arabic with an inimitable peasant accent and like Areúsa's tough in *The Spanish Bawd*, sported a face furrowed by scars and bruises—he invited us both to his sanctuary and I communed simultaneously and in turn with both, whilst Abdelkadir fanned the flames of his own and our pleasures with ejaculatories and quotations from my breviary. (As the *miles gloriosus* later told me, he took him back to the home of an old nonbeliever with whom he'd agreed beforehand the price for his brokerage and the heavenly favors offered.)

In the early eighties, he befriended a young French teacher, who was apparently attempting to catechize Iranians in flight from the Revolution. The apprentice missionary had photographed him with his ace of spades and balls tied up with a leather ring about to sink his lance into a supine Tunisian. He also showed me the whip with which he disciplined one of his ardent customers who yearned for penitence and mortification. *C'est un vieux con*, he said, *mais j'aime lui faire plaisir.* His ascension in the most extreme circles of New York sanctity would have been spectacular. I have not known another virtuoso so dedicated to the rites of humiliating the flesh and other laudable acts of expiation.

I partook of his readings of the Eucology without foreseeing the impending catastrophe. He once invited me to dine in the house of an absent Frenchman with a mustachioed compatriot, a regular in the station lavatories—or the spiritual stations of the lavatories—for me to serve the apéritif while he cooked. The apéritif didn't come off—the novice didn't come on—and Abdelkadir rectified the failure after a due delay to curse the remiss individual and performed to perfection in the shower his art as a celebrant of the rites of cautery and relief.

The one-syllabled monster ended these unctions. In 1983, in the course of my missions in North America, I could verify *de visu* the panic and carnage caused by the pandemic. I resolved, with the Lord's help, to moderate my fervor and ardent visits to the chapels of the blessed. I saw Abdelkadir in one, *mid-obscena observandi cupidus*, and warned him of the risks that he knew of by hearsay. Nevertheless he decided to meditate with me and, impelled by the imperative tone of his argument, I agreed to follow him to the *cella intima* of a pornoshop where, with a potter's zeal and resolution, I molded his column inches to our joint satisfaction. I paid the settlement and haven't seen him since.

May God in His infinite wisdom and goodness, spare both him and me, the unspeakable horrors of the plague!

Ahmed and Omar

I have yet to describe the liturgy of daily trawling and to-and-froing that intensified as twilight gathered and closing-time at the Gare du Nord lavatories drew nigh. In the main, the congregation comprised thirsty souls anxious to be drenched and impregnated with the fruits of virtue, and strapping youths who forged and foraged, posted there for hours on end—strolled and strutted along the underground galleries of the metro and station platforms—as they exhibited all size of handy manual for meditative contemplation by mere, much-scorned Peeping Toms or by those like me summoned to the Ways of Sanctity. Those who came to satisfy base needs ran quickly from that delicious haven of devotion, whether crossing themselves or not, I know not.

I didn't linger: usually, I met up with an acquaintance and, with a quick wink, he'd hide his utensil in his trouser and we'd head to one of the hotels in the 18th district, the land hospitable to my apostolic zeal; at other times, like an officer, I'd review the line of conscripts presenting arms. I waited until I found a space next to the lustiest or the one most spiritually inflamed and, if he responded to my *dominus vobiscum*, we'd walk up to the platforms, and with the saintly shamelessness urged by our Founder, I proffered secure shelter to his anxieties. With a few exceptions (Abdullah, Abdelkadir and the odd one whose name I forget), I avoided the place's mainstays and preferred to venture on the *terra incognita* of the new arrivals.

Ahmed was one of these episodic visitors: his centurion's face and the flame of his votive candle obeyed the Code of Sanctity and the encounter bore us both fruit. Charmed by my intercession, the hesitant flame of his *flambeau* lifted into that measured, burnished expression of firm but friendly charity recommended by Monsignor.

In the *après-lit* chat—no coffee, no sugar-lumps!—he told me he lived in a workers' hostel in Levallois and invited me to visit whenever I felt like it after working hours. I jotted down his address and soon called by: I knocked on his door-number, but somebody else opened up. "Are you the Spaniard?" he asked me in Arabic. I said I was and while he brewed tea in his four-bunk cubby-hole (three made up and one for their cases), he introduced himself (his name was Omar) and suggested replacing his friend in prayers (I had noted his good disposition moments earlier). I was tempted by the unexpected offer: but "Don't we run the risk of Ahmed catching us?" "We're brothers," he assured me, "we share everything." We took off our trousers and officiated in one of the bottom bunks. Omar wasn't such a good lad as his countryman but turned in a clean, serviceable job. Given that Ahmed was late and I had to repair to the Cosa's headquarters, he suggested I return on Sunday morning to commune and lunch with them. As soon as one went to the market, the other would help me. Then, at desserts, oracles would change: each to his own and God on all sides.

And so it went on for several weeks with the Lord's blessing. Ahmed and Omar behaved warmly towards me, joked in Arab dialect, had fun fixing shifts for our splendid union and their respective services. Sometimes, after the litanies, they were visited by other compatriots and I felt at ease in their smoke-filled, packed oratory, immersed in an atmosphere propitious for contemplating the divine mysteries—*et in meditatione mea exardescit ignis*—linked to my brothers in virtuous tasks of edification with bonds impossible even to imagine in my country that has been not only mingy but downright hostile, from the time of the Martyr Saint Pelayo's First Chronicles, to these august works of saintliness. My missions with the sons of Saint Augustine's Numidia and Mauritania Tingitana were enriched and perfected from the day I didn't need to have recourse to the *lingua franca* to communicate with them: we moved in a common arena where my awesome vocation and assiduous reading of the modern Kempis nurtured my pastoral labors, the grace and simplicity of unmediated apostolacy.

My relation with Ahmed and Omar, workers in the nearby car factory in Levallois, encompassed two whole years. As a result, I discovered the harsh, hazardous living conditions in the immigrant workers' quarters: their overcrowding and promiscuity; the regular trawling, from door to door, of women from their land and aged French women; the first appearances of white-capped, bearded proselytizers bearing Korans and the holy books of their sect (May God illumine their souls and point them to the Truth of the Roman, Catholic and Apostolic Church!).

I had sent him a photo of me in the Cosa's headquarters in Ann Arbor, where I preached for a few weeks, and, on my return, I found it stuck to the wall of his room, next to those of Um Kalsoum and the King of Morocco. We reestablished Sunday liturgy: shopping, lunch, coffee, interspersed with devotions and prayers. Then I met Ali and changed my country of mission. As I discovered later, Ahmed returned to his village and Omar, promoted to overseer for his loyal services to the company as a strikebreaker, lived in Clichy. I tried to see them one day but the concierge hailed me. After checking their names and surnames, he told me they weren't on the list of lodgers.

The Well-Endowed

On several occasions, as a Cosa dignatory and to bear witness, I've often visited the country of the W.E., that beautiful region which supplied the French economy hundreds of workers during the boom years of the sixties. Welcomed with open arms by the bosses and overseers in construction sites and factories, at that time the immigrants received papers in order, with the honorable mention that they were "privileged residents" (I had only the most "ordinary" resident's card!).

The Quartier Goutte d'Or was awash with immigrants made of that saintly stuff which kindles the fire of the faithful. They'd gather there after work and on public holidays to chat, exchange news, play cards and listen to musicians from their countries. First with Mohammed and later with his fellow countrymen, I got acclimatized, imbued by missionary spirit, to the cafés on the rue Polonceau, rue de la Charbonnière, rue Stephenson, where the W.E. lived as if on home territory. Following the exemplary Saint Juan de Barbès-Rochechouart, I became a scribe for some and a colleague for others. Their openness to my holy industry and natural inclination to succor grief-stricken souls with that "mace of powerful steel, sheathed in a padded glove" mentioned by our Founder mingle in my memory with sounds of music from Oran which we used to listen to before or after matins.

I later visited the towns and villages of their land in the company of Mohammed and Lakdar. Frequent contact with Europe mitigated the rustic roughness of their ways without undermining their native ferocity. I don't know how many W.E. I outdid in endurance: surely more than twenty. My pious impatience (inspired doubtless by touches from the Paraclete) produced its fruits: aridity and dryness of the senses gave way to the sudden, prolonged expansions of ardent, enraptured souls.

(I don't know if two unruly, unforgettable colossi, imprinted *ad vitam* on my hymnal, the ones I helped out of a tight spot, whose fervors I pacified on my pastoral visits and nocturnal adorations along the boulevards, belonged to the tribe: a brawny giant, extravagantly mustachioed, to whom I dedicated my prayers in a hotel on the rue Clignancourt, in a modest oratory with a double bed, bidet and basin. His vast hands grabbed me by the neck and asked quite seriously: "Aren't you afraid I'll do you in?" I told him it'd be a glorious martyrdom, an imitation of Christ and definitive proof of my saintliness, and he burst out laughing. After his vigorous shafting, he held me tight and slept until dawn. Despite my desire to rejoin and intensify prayers with such a miracle-worker, I failed to trace him on my painstaking trawls of Barbès. I evoke him over time as a dazzling theophany. What can have become of him?

The other saint was walking alone, at a late hour, towards the Stalingrad metro station, and immediately accepted the suggestion we should pray matins together. His passion for possession knew no bounds. He allowed me no shuteye, no truce. The noise of the overland train rattled us at two a.m. Sadly I abandoned the linen threshing ground that was chapel to our *venite adoremus* and *tantum ergo*. I never chanted the prayers in my Breviary with such a feeling of holy release!)

Mustapha was a member of the circle of the W.E.: tall, robust, with a hairless gladiator's chest and prominent facial features that I'm trying to configure mentally without the help of a photograph. We met in the Gare du Nord although he wasn't a frequent visitor to those temples of convenience. Nor did he drink or smoke. Close contact over more than a year revealed to me his sincere, affectionate nature. He didn't dally with his compatriots in the cafés of Barbès and, when we became friends, we established a blessed

Sunday ritual: brunched in a couscous restaurant, coupled in the hotel on the rue Ramey. We went to wrestling bouts at the Elysée Montmartre. And occasionally stopped to chat with my friend Genet in the fairy Café des Oiseaux—I'm not sure their feathers were Saint John of the Cross or Havana's—in the shadow of García Lorca and Severo.

I was his scribe and mentor through the bureaucratic labyrinth of the plan to reunite families: he'd rented a room in a half-ruined building in order to demand a new abode for himself and his own and, after lots of hassle, was successful. When I crossed paths with Iblis, I broke off our relationship abruptly: I exchanged—*stultorum infinitus est numerus*—our pure, pristine meadow for a spinney of nettles and brambles. When I saw Mustapha ten years later we'd both changed. He resided with his offspring in a dilapidated tower block and I'd broken with Sheitan (praised be Our Redeemer!). He told me he was going to drive back to his country in a second-hand car he'd recently acquired and took my advice on routes to Almería and Málaga. His wife and children listened silently to our conversation. I was, according to him, the deputy director of his building firm and they all gazed respectfully at this so-called non-believer boss who spoke Arabic. I haven't seen him since and I wish him a long and happy life.

Saleh was lively and well-equipped. He kneeled on me in bed or bunk on a level with my arms and poured out his carrot-juice while I spurred on his devotions by rubbing mine in his inner chamber. We used to go to Madame Madeleine's busy temple on the Impasse Villa de Guelma and, later, to the Voltaire hammam. As he avoided promiscuity and contact with other souls longing for his spiritual teachings, our prayers continued after the cruel death blows dealt by the one-syllabled virus. I alternated the rough and the rapturous with him and Ali until the day when the public works company he worked for sent him and other laborers from his land to Saudi Arabia. His postcards arrived in the Cosa's Post Box, and I responded by return. Unfortunately, he turned up one Sunday, unexpectedly, in the baths where I was at prayer with my Turk. Caught in flagrant infidelity, I apologized and made a date for the following day. But, as I feared, he didn't show up. I then learned he'd moved to Nancy with his family that had arrived from Morocco.

It's been years since I saw the W.E. but I dream of them. God has furnished them with the finest physical and spiritual qualities he grants his saints. How can one not believe in His infinite Goodness and Wisdom after visiting their beautiful country and relishing the firm vocation of its children in their countless hymns and jubilations?

Ali

Guided by my love for charitable works and for helping souls in distress, I extended my preaching to the Turks. Their providential arrival in Paris at the end of the seventies was a Revelation from the Lord of the infinite variety of His Ways.

I caught first sight of them from a hotel window on the rue Ramey—where a saint of mine had burned bright the coals of virtue hidden beneath the warm embers—chatting in a group on the pavement opposite. Who were those lads and mustachioed males and which language did they speak? My thoughts flew to St. Augustine's precious pages on divine language, the Founding Word which created the universe: that *Fiat lux* which I later modified when I discovered the foreigners had come to my missionary territory contracted by a branch of Volkswagen.

How could I address them if they were totally ignorant of the language of Voltaire and of the Marian Revelations of Lourdes? Their pride and inscrutablity daunted me. For some weeks, I was content to keep them in view as they visited my territory and huddled together on the pedestrian avenue of the boulevard of boulevards. I bought a Turkish dictionary and tried to memorize greetings and polite formulas before embarking on more practical, substantial areas of knowledge.

God guided my way to the new species of *homo voluptarius*: while ruminating in the Gare du Nord lavatories, I discovered a *vir provocator* whose carefully sculpted handlebars or coiled whiplash mustache knocked me from my saddle. I noticed he was lingering more than usual and fingering his instrument while keeping a completely straight face. He pretended not to notice my veneration: prolonged his up and down movements, as if absorbed in the contemplation of the glazed bowl and the water rushing down the hole. I brushed him with my elbow and gestured to him to follow me. Before my rapture and wonderment he buttoned up, escorted me.

The stretch of road to the oratory on the rue Ramey passed in meditative silence: the *çok güzel, biyiklarini seviyorum, yaragin isterim* would come later, as pious practices were perfected and we proved our mutual fervor and devotion. Seared by that love for duty well done that God transmits to His best children, he lubricated, polished, raised his nob to a perfect ovaled finish. We conjugated the verb *sikis* in all its modes and tenses and I didn't stumble over difficult gerunds and participles. The meat was beat twice and thrice, and in the lulls I admired my rider's flaming beauty: the ferocity of his lusty mustache twisting and taking aim like the bayonet of a Hindu infantryman.

(How I thank the Lord for the fleeting hours of fullness He generously grants us in *hac lachrymarum valle!*)

Our joint prayers lasted many a year. In this interlude, I learned to cruise in his language though he never improved his stammering, rural French. He had come contracted by a timber firm and lived in the heart of the woods on the Île de France with a group of compatriots, woodcutters like himself from the city where the remains of Jalaluddin Rumi rest in the mausoleum built in his memory. This happy circumstance—his distance from the society plagued by the pandemic—strengthened my resolve to pray exclusively with him, on the path of prudent souls, anxious to reach the safe harbor in accord with the precepts of our bedtime reading ("Don't fail to enter every sagrarium when you see the walls and towers of the houses of the Lord!").

With the viaticum and safe-pass necessary to survive the storm—cruel hecatomb for so many incautious friends—we sustained and prolonged our novenas in the hotel on the rue Ramey, Madeleine's knocking-shop and the much-lamented baths, site of so much prayer and rapture. After his lively parrying and thrusting, we wandered there along passageways, also frequented by Severo, Roland and the inevitable Saint Juan of Barbès-Rochechouart, watching out for the ergastula where the betrothed of two rosaries of years impatiently awaited the theophany of some well-gifted brawny guard. The gleaming torso of my janissary aroused fear and envy. He was my bodyguard and guardian angel before the virus made inroads in the heat and damp of the bath and inner quiet of the small cells. I continued with him until the vigor of his complexion faded, and after he settled in the Massif Central with his wife and children, he perceptibly reduced my dosage.

(On the threshold of an old age like the one that defeated the mast-head of the hero of *A Cock-Eyed Comedy*, I often evoke the splendor of this Turk, captured in images *sui ipsius nudator*.)

Here end the pages of these Lives of Saints and Their Works, *corrected by their author and destined to direct their readers in their devotions, the original manuscript of which, preciously preserved in the Fondazione Romana Latinitas, can only be consulted by numeraries of the Cosa Santa.*

3 AN INTROIT OUT OF TUNE

Those penetrating pages, those personal experiences of harsh, acerbic devotions are meant for you, discreet reader. Meditate on the lives of those saints and on the multiple access routes to the inner dwelling until their juicy marrow impregnates you.

Imitate Him nailed to the cross. Open yourself like a ploughed furrow to the instrument of tempered steel that brings water, lush green and a harvest of miraculous fruits. Behind each likeness there is a saint to witness your tribulations, anxieties and grief, ready to assuage them with his cauterizing power. Beseech of him staying-power, follow the righteous, cherish their soothing actions. Don't step back: imitate with saintly shamelessness the examples proferred here, ascend to the highest, most speculative mysteries.

In the spring of 1962, after a fruitful period of retreat in the Cosa's House in Rome — where I frequented the future Archbishop of Vienna and other tirelessly zealous souls who have suffered unjust persecution here and will hence inherit the kingdom of heaven — the Vatican executive allotted me a silent, missionary operation in the Mother Land. I reached Barcelona in Archimandrite's cap and ankle-length habit, accompanied only by a Philippine flunky, a discreet helpmate in my domestic chores. Through friends held in common, I had the good fortune to meet the poet, Jaime Gil de

Biedma, a colleague of vast culture and insatiable curiosity, and frequently visited his vast mansion on the Ensanche and private basement apartment in the upper reaches of Muntaner. (He welcomed me on one occasion with cadets from a Greek Navy training-ship and then put an anecdote into circulation that's but a half truth.)

Although I escorted him on his rambles—patrols, inspections, vigils—I preferred to converse with him in the peace and tranquility of his library. Among other manuscripts and incunabula of great value, he preserved a copy of my work printed in Anvers in 1573. He wanted to prise from me new data as to the life of Diego Fajardo, whose loyal services to their cause His Catholic Majesties had rewarded with the concession in perpetuity of the rents from several bawdy-houses, where he exercised his apostolacy in accord with the maxim *occasionem arripere*. The poet was persuaded—and there was no way I could strip him of such a certitude—that a few malign, withering Verses of a Provincial alluded to my holiness. He loved to recite the one which went

Please, Friar Bumble,
a dick ill-fancied by folk,
so mightily humble,
a real bleeding soak,
tell your brother, no fool,
— he must brand your bum
—for the prime tool
— it swallows in fun

before an audience of religious confrères.

I always kept with me a copy of the Kempis of modern times

and we meditated on the deep meaning of some of my favorite maxims ("Your duty is to be an instrument, big or small, rough or subtle . . . Be an instrument!" or "It hurts, doesn't it!? Of course, it does!, That's precisely why you have been hit there"), as a meritorious work accruing great favors. We also recited the *inter medium montem pertransibu penis* and other ejaculatories rich in indulgences. The circle of devotees gathered around Gil de Biedma was unique in the bereft Spain of the time: it was a storehouse of vocations and talents, whose fruit only surfaced much later.

I was keen to preach in lands propitious to my apostolacy and discover treasures of hidden saintliness: fulcra able to relieve burdens and alleviate guilt with the width and vigour of their stout virtue. After acknowledging my dryness and disinclination to labor in zones where he honed his natural saintly gifts, the poet advised me to follow the example of his writer colleague Juan Goytisolo, whose preaching by example had exalted him, so went the whisper, to peaks of perfection. Though I lamented his Peeping Tommery and brazen tendency to appropriate chapters from my diary, I learned much from the words and deeds of his mission. He guided me to the chapels where I found my most fervent catechists and I believe he deserves to be proclaimed, as Severo Sarduy proposed on behalf of the Sisters of Perpetual Succor, Saint Juan of Barbès-Rochechouart.

I advise the reader of this work of devotion to meditate long and hard on its examples and insights that will lead him, along steep paths of enduring merit, to the ardent, succulent glories of the Chosen.

4 MANUSCRIPT II: THE SECRET DWELLINGS

1

The reading of these lives of saints—written for the meditation and recreation of souls—would be incomplete without a detailed description of the temples where the former exercised their apostolacy: men short on prayer and long in action, following our Founder's maxim, rid themselves there of dead weight, of terrestrial dross, raised the majesty of their scepters in the live flame of love!

The chapels they frequented spread like a brilliant constellation across the dark city sky. From Pigalle to the overground metro station of Stalingrad they formed an often broken line gently branching out to those circular, dimly lit sanctuaries, where the devout sought "inspiration from the saints" and spiritual cautery.

A cardboard moon and imitation stars hung over the slate roofs, the pillars and girders supporting the metro, the arcades under which expresses and suburban trains passed, the still, opaque waters of the canals: that whole array of elements cleverly arranged as in a figure in a school textbook. The mean-spirited light embellished with a mysterious halo the cracked, hungover façades, the one-eyed, bleary, twisted looks of Paris's old buildings infiltrated by immigrant cafés and dives, the seventh pillar and fifth column of God's secret designs.

The Sisters of Perpetual Succor stumped from oratory to oratory without flinching at the cold or inclement weather, or waited deeply meditative, in that faith the Lord grants the creatures He loves, the sudden appearance of some saint (as our Kempis puts it, "Are you not happy if you discover another tabernacle on your way though the city's streets?").

For years I witnessed impassioned ejaculatories, acts of love and amends, binding communions. Faithful to the imperative mandates of the missionary tasks of my apostolacy, I dallied evening and night around the chapels, watched entrances and exits, until I encountered a friend or stranger ready to join me in prayer.

(From the discreet haven of old age, I now relay the faces and attributes of some saints I didn't mention in the first part of this book:

A wise Algerian hillsman, with voracious lips and wild mustache, whose proud staff soared solemn as a steeple. With him "the great desire for 'this' to work and dilate," of which our Founder speaks became a succulent "impatience." He chewed, twirled this mustache, angrily pressed the erogenous zones of aspirants after his graces while dexterously plunging in his instrument, leaving lees, transmuting pain into yearned-for bliss. I often found him round the cottages on the boulevard Rochechouart by the entrance to the Anvers metro. These two homilies fit him like a bishop's ring on an oblate's finger: "By your example and your word produce the first circle, then another, another, and another, ever widening out" and "The desire will not be in vain if we unleash it in coercive action with saintly shamelessness." Sayed Lunes—such was his name—also favored Saint Juan of Barbès-Rochechouart with his heavenly gifts. His unquenchable zeal soothed and lubricated both.

A mechanic whose sturdy neck, prominent nose and bulbous ears, like cauliflowers or carnivorous flowers, remind me of those belonging to my wrestler friend from Smyrna. He consoled the blessed souls of the Nocturnal Adoration. He lived in a hut in the Stalingrad area where he got horny and still proffered his bitter cup to all distressed souls in an inexhaustible desire to proselytize.

Dominus dabit verbum evangelizantibus virtute multa.)

Immigrant Paris, its back turned on the grandiose museum of the City of Lights, warmly welcomed my contemplative cruising. Genet lodged in one of its hotels between journeys to the refugee camps of Jordan and the Lebanon. Apart from him and my diligent scribe, I never bumped into any acquaintance of mine in that extra-territorial Vatican. The three-roomed, glass-roofed tabernacles—where some punctilious devotees deposited loaves later to be consumed with unction, irrigated by the virtue of the clientèle—were felled by a cruel, arbitrary death sentence. Infinite opportunities for worship for apostles of standing and substance suddenly disappeared and the Sisters of Perpetual Succor were unable to organize a single procession or funeral like those for the urinal on the Rambla immortalized in *The Thief's Journal.* May I see those responsible for such vandalism—Giscard, Chirac and the whole gang—burn in the seventh, most horrendous circle of those condemned to Gehenna! I will never recover from their barbaric destruction.

2

As Saint Juan of Barbès tells it to his scant though fervent disciples, one fine day he was visited in his flat by a svelte, grey-eyed, fair-haired youth, whose angelic appearance, harbinger of good fortune or ill, left a deep impression. He had come to offer him two photos of Genet, sitting on a park bench in Rabat, taken a few days before his demise. "I know he was a close friend of yours, and bring them to you as a memento." While he effused words of gratitude, the archangel spoke of Roland Barthes whom he'd also snapped, by chance, on the eve of his fatal collision. My memoirist eyed the youth rather anxiously, glowing in his aura of inner light, and anxiety transformed to panic when he added, gently and benignly: "Today it's your turn." A stentorian NO resounded around his home. The angel departed taking his enigma with him; nevertheless the celestial aroma from his apparition lingered on and Saint Juan of Barbès had to open the balcony window and air his flat though it was winter and gusts of wind stirred infinite flurries of snow over Paris and its attics.

I got to know the semiologist in the Luxor Cinema, a tabernacle of supreme sanctity and haven for my apostolic missions. The devotees who hastened to the temple never left disappointed. As our infallible pilgrims' guide says, "What beauty in their fruits! what maturity in their works!" The action was intense, especially on the *festi dies ludorum*. The saints were ready for anything in the upper reaches—where they shafted shamelessly without a backward glance, in the jostling throng of passageways, and basement lavatories—a real hive of busy bees and drones inning and outing, stings ever at the ready to elongate and hook in. It would take more than the Acts of the Apostles to relate the succession of laudable deeds and countless prodigies within this human industry. Gay cats of the *gai savoir* wilfully guyed their gay gordons: a moll, past philandering, with polka-dot bathrobe and hair-slide; a New York mulatta, "with splendorous butt." R.B. roamed the holy places elegantly elated: he saw, he conquered, he came like Caesar; nodding appreciatively to members of the club addicted to this Parnassus of fishers of men.

Upon his death (may the Lord welcome him mercifully to His bosom!), a mutual friend dispatched to me a few paragraphs from his diary where he'd noted his visits to that peculiar Mecca of a cinema with a commitment clearly emblematic of his saintly stature. I'll copy them exactly as I received them for the future edification of our brothers in the apostolate.

Fragments from the Semiologist's Diary

Saturday 20 Take the underground to Barbès after lunch with F. and Severo. Cinema bursting at the seams. Lots of action in the upper circle and basement. Some drag queens. *Deux fois.*

Wednesday 31 A fine uproar in the pit. An usherette turned her flashlight on a Sister kneeling between the legs of a black. "I'm fed up with seeing you crawling on the floor," etc. The Sister, unperturbed: "It's not the quality of your films that brings me here." The manager came to sort it out.

18 May Lots of lovely blacks in the loos. People strike deals, go in and out quickly. You can see lots of trousers dropping under the doors to the stalls.

7 June The cinema again. Karate, kung fu. Activity on two fronts: on the screen and in the stalls. Met up with the crazy Lascar with the scar.

Saturday 19 Police raid. The hens and cocks had to scamper from the chicken-run.

No date Goddess H. Luxor Cinema. *Deux fois.* Get home exhausted.

J.G. was also an habitué of this *sancta sanctorum* where, resurrected like Lazarus, the sempiternal Bruce Lee triumphed daily. Unlike the Semiologist, he has left us a description—for once not inspired by my writings!—of that castle of piety where the Sisters of Perpetual Succor accumulated good works and fulfilled goals rich in indulgences, vying in the fervor of their priestly supplications. Though they divert me somewhat from my didactic path, I will reproduce a few paragraphs, while craving the forgiveness of readers of this manual of devotion.

The Luxor was a true movie palace, with single-priced seats in stalls, balcony and gallery and motley audiences with a passing interest in what was happening on screen: the real plot developed for many in the basement and dress-circle bathrooms, the upper rows of the mezzanine and whole of the gods. The habitués were mostly immigrants and a faithful, variegated minority, of those Friar Bugeo exalts to the category of blessed: from the dyed Philippine, with fan and hair-comb, to R.B. the semiologist. Some of the clientèle never got into the frequently fascinating story of the films being shown: their goals were other. When an intrepid compatriot extended her manual activities to the center of the stalls only to be caught *in flagrante* by the usherette's flashlight, she responded regally to the attendant ousting her: "Naturally, that's what I'm after, not the lousy films you put on!"

Rival gangs in synchronized confrontations, karatekas in stupendous leaps and flights, adversaries eliminated one by one from bottom to top following a pyramidal hierarchy: what delights for my Maghreb friends and myself. The films' thematic simplicity, the clear distinction between the righteous and the wicked, helped them escape a world where the hazy frontiers between exploiters and exploited masked a real perception of the reasons for their exile and alienation. While I registered the rules of the game of the genre, they celebrated and applauded the winner's predictable feats. But, though my interest was of a different nature, it was genuine and fused with the immigrants' in warm, harmonious communion. Every artistic genre spawns its own parody and karate was no exception. A few anarchists imbued with the

festive spirit of May '68 bought the rights to a Taiwanese film, produced a soundtrack more to their taste and fixed its distribution on the
cinema circuit packed by North Africans. Its title, *The Dialectic Can
Break Stones*, apparently mimicked one of Mao's famous sayings. The
pirated plot went more or less like this: a merciless war opposes two
groups of youths, one bureaucratic, one libertarian. The leader of the
latter—let's call him Ling Pi—goes out to fight single-handed
twenty-odd enemies bristling with arms. Miu, his little sister, wants to
go with him, but our hero prevents her: "Your erroneous political line
won't let you accompany me. For once stop reading doorstops by
Marx and Lenin and immerse yourself in de Sade's *Complete Works!*"
The girl walks tearfully off and seeks refuge at home. "Why are you
crying, Miu?," her father asks anxiously. "Ling Pi wouldn't let me go
with him to liquidate the bureaucrats. He says I lack political maturity
and, rather than wasting my time on Communist classics, I should
study the Marquis de Sade." "Well, too true, Miu honey. A young girl
will get much more from reading *The 120 Days of Sodom* than Marx's
endless stodge."

The next sequence shows Ling Pi in full possession of his karateka
arts, decimating the ranks of bureaucrats with well-targeted blows
from his forearm: "Idiots, stop parroting the editorials of *L'Humanité!*"
The rival leader: "Revisionist, traitor!" Ling Pi: "Now you'll see the
strength of a disciple of Nietzsche and Lou Andreas Salomé," etc.

Needless to say, the film delighted me. But it also delighted the rest
of the audience in the stalls who, absorbed by the wondrous incidents
on screen, paid little attention to the Sisters' wheeler-dealing or to the
jokes and piquant dialogue.

The Luxor Cinema was an unforgettable breeding ground for
saints and the hallowed. Whether before or after the onslaught of
the single-syllabled monster, that "offspring of angry demons
thirsty for animal lymph" of which Sarduy writes so beautifully, I
know not—but its unexpected closure was a blow from which its

parishioners have yet to recover. When on one of my now rare sorties in the neighborhood I see its art nouveau façade ravaged by time and cruel, mercantile indifference, my soul and all else hanging in there shrivel. It was where I found respite from desolation and conferred relief on many a meritorious nob and sod. It was where I exhorted catechists to follow the words in our guide and breviary: "Can you not see how you are so small that in life you can but offer those small crosses?" They harkened and the pain brought by the Saint's stern severities was soon transmuted into blissful peace.

3

According to our Holy Roman, Apostolic, Catholic Church the existence of hell, and consequently of Satan and his bellicose legion of devils, is a solid, incontrovertible truth, sustained by numerous conciliar resolutions and encyclicals. Only dustily wigged freethinkers and outmoded liberals excoriated by our Founder would today dare deny an axiom corroborated by the most modern advances in science, for fear of looking ridiculous. Embodied in the beautiful, sensual Salomé, one of these malign spirits tempted Herod Antipas until she obtained the Baptist's head, another seduced me in the Luxor loos.

Iblis was tall, swarthy, robust, muscled like a Turkish champion wrestler, and a doodad most keen to enter the fray. Misfortune led me to bump into him during an afternoon showing, when I went down to the basement to exercise my apostolic zeal and found him hands on hips, parading his pride and joy, up for the best offer. He performed standing up, serene and sure of his vigor. I saw him as a model of virtue and sanctity (*ideo omnia sustineo propter electos*), and after an exchange of mutually satisfactory services, I invited him to a coffee on a boulevard terrace.

Iblis artfully concealed his affiliation to the Malign One and succeeded in submitting me to his domination for over two years. He charged top dollar for his favors and insisted on a one-sided loyalty. He was harsh, jealous, manipulative, possessive. He parried and thrust in narrow confines never leaving the breech or surrendering it up in acts of docile genuflection. It was his fault that I abandoned my missionary labors, neglected prayers and ejaculatories, forgot my duties towards God and His Divine Intercessor: the cult of dulia towards the saints metamorphosed into one of latria, contrary to the most basic ecclesiastical principles. I thought erroneously that I was following the maxims of our Kempis ("Put your miserable head to his breast opened so his heartbeats may drive you mad"); but (this was the *quid pro quo*) he was not one of the Lord's chosen, but a temptor sent by the Enemy. And so I stopped visiting chapels and going to churches, left promises and precepts unfulfilled, switched from sowing seed to sucking at straws. Iblis was the graveyard of true piety and my secular record as an Archimandrite. Majestic, even grandiose in his disguise, he led me to the edge of the abyss where reprobates burn eternally by the Holy Will of God. Although "anyone can err in life," I will never cease to repent of my sins and wrongdoings.

(Reader: don't worry if, as you consider the works of my saints, you hesitate before following in their steps, fearful you won't attain the grace of so much wonder and prodigy.

My notepad is a vademecum to open sanctums and slip into their mysterious reaches. Sow and be sure the seed will take root and bring forth fruit. The harvest is rich and reapers few.)

4

The convents of Ávila, where petite nuns spend their free time between chants and prayers manufacturing small whips and scourges to mortify the flesh in pursuit of a healthy soul, began in the seventies to receive numerous orders from abroad, particularly from Amsterdam, San Francisco and Manhattan. The ropes or switches lovingly plaited into whips of differing shape and hardness—to fit the different stations of penitents in their ascesis—attracted a growing trade, clients whose devotion manifested itself in the need for novel, more savage instruments of torture: belts, studded leather straps and bracelets, collars, gauntlets, lashes and flails. Mother Superiors and Abbesses couldn't contain their joy: even in those times of tepid faith and disbelief, virtue was purifying its labors and extending its territory. The delicate, white, almost translucent hands, made for telling beads and making cakes, buns, marzipan whirls and other delicious tidbits, swopped sugar for aloes and shaped tools destined to tame passions and stiffen weak, wavering souls. The orders from shops selling holy objects on Christopher Street and other sanctuaries of New York piety rained down daily. Impossible to supply the needs and desires of the faithful: the harvest of souls outstripped the most optimistic forecasts. "Fight off spiritual aridity and low ebbs! Heed the advice of the blessed and let your expert hands nurture into the light a thousand flowers of virtue, a thousand buds of sanctity!": the confessor to one of the convent Mother Superiors, informed by a common friend won over by my silent preaching by example in North American territories—where I studied for a Masters in Business Sciences and Soul Merchandising—exhorted me to encourage adepts of extreme ardors to persevere in their fine work and not yield in their efforts until Communism fell and Russia was converted according to the prophecies of Our Lady of Fatima.

(The prophecy was fulfilled late and, although plunged into sudden, cruel, earthly poverty, the Russians have saved their souls. Yet nobody highlights the role played there by the expiatory discipline and self-punishment of S & M activists.)

I was witness to the good works and travails described by the confessor in my apostolic meanderings though the West Village and environs of Forty-second Street. I wasn't carrying my usual guide to the Holy Places published by Spartacus: I abandoned myself to that delicate diviner, the instinct the Lord grants those who love Him. Although my preaching never went beyond contemplative meditation to action through a dearth of the saints I favored in my devotions, I was able to appreciate the collective fervor and longing in the baths, cinemas and backrooms of pornoshops.

I can now recall:

The bathhouse in Saint Mark's Place where, in a potpourri of races, swaddled in white bathrobes, the parishioners wandered like spirits or souls in distress between cubicles with padded bunks, refuge of the sorrowful blessed waiting for saints to perform. Those already graced by their favors recovered from the deed in a dormitory of barrack or hospital proportions after curfew and evening prayers. Individuals wandered between beds of joy or pain, bowed solicitously, anxious to cauterize or soothe the wounded.

The cinema on Fourteenth Street, a few blocks from Union Square, where lights never illumined shadowy boxes, stairways, stalls and circle: there was a continuous showing and groups of the faithful gathered in uninterrupted prayer. I'm unsure whether Severo Sarduy's Sisters of Succor or Support frequented these haunts, no doubt very familiar to Nestor, Reinaldo and Saint Juan of Barbès-Rochechouart.

The empty shell of the Customs House on the Hudson River quayside, the mooring-point and destination of boats crammed with immigrants in flight from hunger, pogroms and wars filmed by Chaplin and Elia Kazan. When I visited there, it was the rendezvous for souls fond of the darkness that hid their earnest labors. Only God, all-seeing, all-hearing, could list and describe such holy industry!

The Mine Shaft, with its old tunnels, galleries, cages and pits. Modern lighting reinvented there the harsh torments suffered at the hands of our blessed Inquisitors in days of yore: a shadowy scenario of racks, shackles, chains and leather hoods, dimly candlelit, like the Cosa's chapels for Spiritual Exercises or Ignatius of Loyola's children in his cave in Manresa (Catalunya, Spain). The whips lashed relentlessly. Blood, sweat and tears flowed to wailing, groaning, and swooning.

I entered, saw, and departed. Hence I am still alive.

(One sunny morning, Divine Providence contrived to test me on a park bench in Washington Square. I was enjoying a break between my classes of theodicy and hip hermeneutics when a swarthy, sturdy youth, with a halo and all the external signs of a saint, flopped down beside me. He was holding—I saw it out of the corner of my eye—an English translation of the book of Muslim revelation which he began to leaf through. I addressed him in his prophet's tongue, but he retorted: Sorry, I don't speak Arabic. Where did he hail from? I'm American. Disappointedly I switched language and we spoke awhile and his personal charms endured. I finally left him—had to get back to my students—and scrawled my address on a piece of paper. Days later, as night fell—by then I'd forgotten the encounter and the saint—the telephone rang. It was him and he was waiting in the lobby. I rushed down not giving it a moment's thought and rashly followed him into a car waiting for us nearby. He introduced me with a here he is! to the occupants—the driver and two friends whose dark faces I could scarcely make out—and we slowly made for an unknown destination. I was beset by vague anxieties: who were these silent strangers with whom I was heading who knows where? How had I come to fall into such a ridiculous trap? They were all quiet and the silence deepened as we drove towards Harlem. My dubious mentor responded monosyllabically to my inane questions. The journey lasted centuries until the car halted opposite a shadowy apartment block. I got out with the others who escorted me to the entrance to a building. The lift took us to a flat where half a dozen guests were congregated around a table laden with all manner of juice and mineral drink, but no alcohol. The mystery was no more. They were Black Muslims. They wanted to talk religion with me. I participated with a sigh of relief and, thanks to the inspiration of the Holy Spirit, I emerged strengthened from my test. Those blessed with eternal glory must surely have appreciated my defense of the Trinity and other dogmas established on solid scientific bases by a long line of Councils and Pastorals from our Mother Church.)

Years later, the pandemic swept through those temples of devotion. The Lord, in His infinite Goodness, aggravated the suffering and torments of the Sisters of Perpetual Succor to the point of supreme expiation, thus granted them right of entry to heaven. But, by virtue of the designs of His also infinite Wisdom, He deprived me (may He be blessed a thousand times!) of that cruel, brutal torture and kept me in this base world on the lookout for fresh opportunities to visit my charitable fervors on select souls.

5

After my exercises and prayers, I'd sometimes sit myself down in the bathhouse's Moorish salon, inaugurated, according to the Governess, by Napoléon le Petit and the Empress Eugénie, and converse with colleagues who, like me, were regular attendees.

(I won't describe the place, as inevitably J.G. from Barcelona already has, and I'd find it quite toe-curling to take yet another slice of his bacon.)

The red-headed Governess poured us mint tea while she kept an eye on her customers' comings and goings over the top of her specs. At the next table, still in a sweat, Sisters Succor and Support fanned themselves with great flourishes. Between gin fizzes they compared the merits and holy ways of the fisty and feisty saints whose prayers they'd just answered.

"What a whopper!" said one.

"My knees are still all a-tremble!" sighed the other.

(Saint Juan of Barbès very rarely came to these *conversazione*: he'd walk the upstairs passages with his Turk or some other rough. The Semiologist also mortified his flesh hereabouts and fulfilled the exigencies of his apostolic mission.)

My friends Severo and Néstor questioned me about the obscure centuries of my life, from the printing of *A Cock-Eyed Comedy* to my reappearance in Jaime Gil de Biedma's circle of friends as an Archimandrite and Cosa zealot: was it true I visited Saint Juan of the Cross in his Toledan prison and kept a secret correspondence with Saints Teresa and Juan of Ávila? What were my cock-eyed adventures under the Hapsburgs and Bourbons during our country's period of terminal decline? Did I meet the Sevillian canon Don José María Blanco White y Crespo during his sojourn in Cadiz or in his definitive exile to Britain? On another occasion while we chatted with two Cosa colleagues keen on meditation and some queens fond of bell-pulling, Néstor plucked from his sleeve a copy of the *Song Book* recently printed in Spain and read aloud a couple of verses from "Juvera's Chamber" and the "Dispute of the Veil." I'll reproduce them for the benefit of the pious souls who will read this book:

Every thigh in the vicinity
by Moors lies besieged
and a turret defeated
from the times of the Trinity . . .

Everything that must enter
and keep inside another
has to be ready ever
to be an inner and outer
in every sweet encounter.

He also liked to recite the "Verse of Count de Paredes to Juan the Poet when captured by Moors from Fez" or a passage from the "Provincial." As for Severo—with the inseparable Succor and Support—he had rewritten and adapted to his much-lamented Cuban landscape one of the devout biographies from my Eucology. I lovingly preserve the paragraph he penned:

The Guanabacoa Tunnel, by the name of María de la O, is from Camagüey and is well acquainted with the Island's *santeros*. She's on the Central Committee with Dalia and other courtesans. I think she is now retired and is Emeritus Professor from the University of Dong. She opted for the nickname because, though blessed from birth and always loyal to her nature, for many a year nobody crossed her threshold because of the mighty Roca (not Blas, by the way) who defended her, until a holy Calabar from Regla, known as the Templer of Steel, artfully found a path, and ever since the way has much widened, so much so, that two carts can now pass and not be a hindrance. She met the Plan's every target and was hoisted high by the clerical arm as an exemplary teacher. The one who suffered, conquered! *Voluntas suficit.*

But the episode in the book which aroused most passion and zeal—the object of a thousand erudite glosses and commentaries—concerned Satilario and the devil who inadvertently perched on his member. Who was Satilario? Was he someone I invented or did I know him via his works?

"Struggle against the weakness which renders you lazy and listless in your spiritual life," enjoins our Kempis. And Satilario concocted the remedy, the bitter cup we must drink to the dregs in order to crown the edifice of sanctification. Comforted by these readings, we spread ourselves around the baths, the restroom, the small cells on the top floor, eager for new opportunities for good works. The staff's keen, penetrating faith warmed and encouraged us on the way to holy shamelessness. There I did pray canonical prayers countless times with my janissary.

Afterwards, as a result, great, nay, prodigious things came to pass between him and me which it would be prolix to explain.)

and 6

Finally, I found my center, dwelling and delight and, soon after I'd reached there, I met the Bard. My guide was M., a veteran from the colonial expeditionary force in Indochina, captured by the Vietcong after the defeat of the French and released after the signing of the Vietnamese independence accords. He then returned to his country of birth with a modest pension and a natural, genial inclination to wile and guile as a go-between. He first escorted me to the capital where, thanks to his skilful groundwork, I was put in touch with half a dozen Red Berets whose memory I cherish most pleasantly as well as a colleague from prison coarse in tongue, a sharp-pointed whipper with whom, in deepest agony, I recited prayers on an unforgettable night of *miserere et retribue dignare* on which he repeated: "You wanted it, then you shall have it." (The Barcelona memoirist novelized him and the member poking out of his P.E. shorts, by plundering the diaries I ingenuously entrusted to him on one of my trips to missionary lands as a Cosa legate.)

The Goliard was a giant with a shaven head and ruddy countenance: when I saw him amid the Square's hustle and bustle, I mentally composed the oration: *tu vero homo unanimis dux meus at notus meus, qui simul mecum dulces copiabas cibus.* Minutes later he was in my bed, led by M.'s hand. The furniture in the rented flat creaked and shook as he entered because every human endeavor proclaims and praises the miracles of our Maker. M. discreetly slipped off for a stroll and I was left alone with him.

Rocket—for that was how he was known—notably lived up to his nickname by dint of his awesome combination of strength and height. His wit and verbal flair had no end. He targeted everything and always hit bull's eye. His gifts were supernatural: it was impossible to dismantle the pins and central pole of his tent. It wouldn't fit *per angostam viam* and homage had to be paid outdoors. The structure of his ballistic artifact, its jet-engine and back-up motors, was equal to the total weapon dreamed of by Pentagon strategists from the beginning of the cold war. No lad or lass could resist attack. His deeds and sayings, noted over the years, would fill the pages of a voluminous collection of the *Lives of the Saints*.

I could relate countless exemplary moments from his public sermons and devout, contemplative acts if Saint Juan of Barbès hadn't stuck his big nose in, with characteristic cheek . . .

How do you write a shout? wondered the author of our southern Moll. He didn't find the answer or, if he did, didn't transcribe it: he left us in the lurch. But the shout sounded and resounded: it was recorded. Its power interrupted the writing of the manuscript the reader is now holding. In a conversation with the freeloading Abbot, included in chapter five of this book, Friar Bugeo maliciously fingers its author.

(Editor's note)

5 THE AFTERMATH OF A SHOUT

Someone had lifted a mangy hand to their earlobe, as if to nibble or fondle their telefonino or perhaps merely to adjust their tone of voice like the divas of old: the tremolo thundered upwards from the din of traffic where Alcalá meets the Gran Vía to the upper reaches of the grand building on the corner. The caryatids, cornices and Corinthian columns that adorn the balconies shook. The acoustic shockwave hit the dome and the statue crowning it. Minerva's breasts swayed and quivered. An eyelash dislodged. The gilt bronze crescent moon landed on a dame's startled horsehair hat. A shiver ran through her from head to toe and she raised a hand to her upper story. What was the provenance of such a strange object? She examined in turn clouds, sickly skyscape, the almost anemic sun. It was a day for peculiar happenings. She checked that (having just left a beautician's salon) her facelift hadn't suffered from the descent of the celestial body, waited for the green light from the Alcalá traffic lights, sprinted spryly across the zebra, twisted left, then right and disappeared amid the other visitors bustling in the entrance to the Circle of Fine Arts.

A huge crowd jostled in the foyer, lined up for tickets, went up and down the lifts: the young and not-so-young, a lady of almost three

rosaries of years, a bow-tied hag, two ageless items in grey herring-
bone, their vacuous visages the perfect expression of the idiocy of
a weekend golfer. In vain she sought out a point of light, the raw
blast from Norway, the ecstasy of transfiguring union. She had
drunk two gin fizzes to put herself in the mood and felt trapped in
the slurry of leering leeches: the mass or morass Ortega likes to
lecture on. A strange quotation sprang to mind: "A verdant, voracious cayman swallowed a cobra coiling through the hands of an
Indian god who was gulping down a hummingbird hanging in the
air on a sugar lump, and the bird in turn, attracted by the phospho-
rescent glow, ingested a firefly in one mouthful." Who had written
that extravagant, curlicued sentence? Her gaze hovered involuntar-
ily over a gawb's fish-eyed, blank look. Its viscous presence immo-
bilized it as in a catapult for catching birds. She shut her eyes but,
on reopening them, the guy was still there. She had no option but
to follow him into the lift, to ascend with him. Upstairs, obse-
quious eyes sought contact with the gormless gawb. The audience
awaited the arrival of that famous lecturer!

She looked for a seat in the back row of the stalls and esconced
herself. The gawb's slimy catapult persisted: forced her to look at
the table and the bunch of microphones assembled to catch the
nectar from his lips. Would he hold forth on the Paraclete, the
melting of the polar ice cap, Aristotelian hilomorphism, genetic
engineering or the targets for the recent sugar-cane harvest?
The man acting as master of ceremonies cleared his throat: well,
I must begin by saying—. Someone coughed, laughter rippled
round the room, she felt queasy. It would be the last straw if she
sicked up and spoiled the presentation of the academic and Maître

des Conférences de l'École des Hautes Études, author into-the-bargain of a prize novel, yes siree, one that grabs you by the throat and won't let you go, that makes the heart flutter, takes your breath away, dazes and fazes. Polite applause, like raindrops on a sheen of stagnant water, stirred and perked her up. She powdered her nose and listened: my novel is—and why not? a euro-novel, a euro-novel or novel of the euro, as an embittered young writer recently sniped, a novel with all the ingredients which can be easily digested by refined stomachs because we Europeans of long standing, are privileged or pained, in relation to the Spanish who have just integrated into our culture, *nous avons un foie!*, and that's why we beg you to cherish and keep intact this organ we so much dote on, don't fall for the artifice and complications so dear to your forebears! We have cut all the fat after Rabelais, don't you see? Since then, we've had Madame de Lafayette and Benjamin Constant! In a word, we do not like over-rich dishes! obviously we don't mean that the Spanish novel up to Grasián is inedible and worthless, far be it for us to affirm such a thing contrary to our eclecticism and a betrayal of our principles. But the euro-European is, by God, proud of the euro-novel's reputation and won't let it be challenged by digressions and games, nay by arabesques that we Europeans of long standing . . .

Somebody had disconnected the microphone: the movements of the trembling, semi-detached lower lip of the novelist mirrored a floundering carp's. Suddenly she saw, through the aquarium's glass walls, myriads of colleagues in varying shapes and sizes: their back and tail fins shaking, their eyes bulging, in a state of stupefaction. The body of the orator-fish got entangled in the net. The lecturer was opaque.

The hatted dame shook herself, tried to unglue herself from her seat. The orator-fish (the Maître des Conférences from l'École des Hautes Études) secreted shiny bubbles, cultivated pearls, beads unthreaded from the necklace of a Great Duchess of Spain. She ran between the algae and mutant flowers. The microphone began to work once more: you should forget, like your damned jota, Góngora's opulent baroque quite different to our Western canon and only keep it in mind for the day when some euro-reader from the era of the euro—hoh! hoh! hoh!—eager for local color, asks you to concoct a constipated book like the one by the Caribbean Proust . . . right?

She finally reached the door, breast-stroked through the viscous water, oxygenated her lungs. Checked her horsehair hat was still in place. Rushed towards the lift.

Disarray once more, up and down, down and up, from floor to floor. She let her instincts guide her out of the oppressive cage behind a miss with a mauve, mellifluous mobile—"I shall now comment on the subject of"—into a lobby or central space where she spotted Succor and Support, Severo's soul-mates. Surrounded by culture-hungry fauna, they were waiting for the door advertising Friar Bugeo's press conference to be opened.

Again she chose a back-row seat: she caught sight of an incendiary blonde and fear that her tresses might ignite and burn down the room cautioned her into a place near the exit. She had to be very wary on that day of rapid turn-arounds, climatic depressions and mood-changes. The proximity of a spindly youth, his single eye glinting metallic and inquisitorial, reinforced her misgivings. She enacted a brief exercise in Buddhist self-contemplation. When it ended, the youth had vanished but not his eye.★ It hung from one of the cords on the chandelier like a lethargic balloon-owl. Did it belong to the Omniscient author who had created it? The mere conjecture sent a chill down her spine, filled her with anxiety. A few little fishes, also in flight from the aquarium, floated through the air, puffed out in serene self-sufficiency, like the thoughts of some Hegelian philosopher, a disciple of Kant, but fond of Nietzsche. Then she saw jellyfish or encephalon extracted from the cranial cavity, mollusks tentacularly restless. Or, could they be irate squid ready to shoot their ink? Her head went round and round. She downed a Pyramidon dry. Was she suffering from an infection to the Lalouette pyramid on her thyroid isthmus or to the Malpighi kidney isthmus? There and then she decided to consult her family doctor (with whom she shared her pillow and many other things besides), a sage in matters neurological as well as a pupil of Lacan.

The platform set-up, lit indirectly, was theatrical. Center stage was held by an armchair awaiting Friar Bugeo's wearisome posterior and ruffled bum-fluff and on the left by three panel-members on chairs lined up behind a microphone-laden table: the publisher of the work with which, you, curious reader, are already familiar and critics recently released from the room with the novelist and Maître des Conférences: Iñigo and Miguel Ángel. Gaseous bubbles ascended the dame's trachea to her brain. Her vision blurred: she was back in the goldfish bowl. Or was it a tank on a fish-farm?

★He was Andrei Biely, born in St. Petersburg, the city he immortalized in his novel.

Coral now covered Friar Bugeo's empty chair. Everyone present blew bubbles from their mouths and gills.

"Ladies and gentlemen (he cleared his throat), my intervention in this act, well, in this event, is led by the need (another clearing of the throat) to proffer a polite apology for Friar Bugeo's unexpected absence (mumbling in the auditorium and a rush of bubbles to the ceiling), an absence due (shouts of: it's beeen rigged!) not to the natural indispositions of age but (raising his voice: shouting) to his being banned expressly by the Cosa Santa! (the whistles worsened: the publisher waited for silence to be restored). The Fondazione Vaticana Latinitas has charged him with a mission to the bishopric of Licia and the Friar is awfully sorry (more throat-clearing) but he doesn't have the time, that is, won't, against his best wishes, be able to be with us. I hope you catch my drift (choking on the algae coming out of his mouth), that is why I've come in his place, well (a shoal of little fishes intent on tracing perfect spirals wrapped round him streamer-like, a flying fish flapped in the footlights and shot off into the shadows), to answer your questions and furnish you with information . . ."

The dame with the horsehair hat (who'd quaffed a designer drug in her gin fizz) thought: I am a fish. And was immediately surrounded by brightly covered marine and aquatic species: moon fish, selachians, arborescent reefs, bivalve shells.

There were not yet lizards or birds.

A nearby squid doused her in a thick cloud of ink.

After skimming through the book, the critics pronounced:

It's a total hodge-podge!
No narrative coherence whatsoever!

The structure's contrived, a pastiche!
Hallucinating self-infatuation!
More dithyrambs to machos and hirsute yokels!
That old inane onanist song!
No dramatic progression.
A circular, repetitive text!
Too true, a vicious circle.
Prenez un cercle, caressez-le, il deviendra vicieux!
Who are you quoting?
Ionesco, for fuck's sake!

She dropped off. The fishbowl had transformed into a computer screen with ephemeral flowers, virtual gardens, intergalactic vehicles, the mask of a Quechua warrior with Lanvin rouge and the bloodshot eyes of a clip-joint hostess from Port Sudan.

She woke up and downed a second Pyramidon. The aquarium and its fauna and flora had vanished. Succor and Support winked at her maliciously from the front row. She divined several Sisters in white habits and the Philippine in her risqué miniskirt. The questions from the audience blasted away and exploded against the night sky like ingenious roman candles.

What was known about Friar Bugeo's life during the Dark Ages?

Did he escort don Diego Fajardo's precious relic on its move to the Coliseum in Rome?

Where was his prick preserved today?

Was it still in a convent of the Sisters of Charity or did it enjoy a special space in the Vatican Museum?

How could one account for the longevity of the author of the book that contains us?

(A sarcastic interjection: Bet he's a yogurt-eater! Another, echoing it: Dannon or Yoplait?)

Wasn't it rather a case of transmigration? According to Pythagoras and the Hillozite dissidents . . .

(This speech was booed.)

Had he shared Gil de Biedma's basement on Muntaner, as black as its reputation?

Why did he hang up his Archimandrite habits for the lay garb of the Cosa Santa?

Does he intend to continue afflicting us with his tales of holy pick-ups?

The publisher meringued like the white of an egg beaten with sugar: splayed on the table, melted, oozed all over, dripped off the edge in big dollops. A hummingbird slipped in through the half-open door and, after tracing a hieroglyph, disappeared the same way. Succor and Support went in hot pursuit. A group of spectators rushed the exit. But there was no fire or threat of fire.

(The incendiary blonde wasn't for burning.)
There was nothing: nothing at all.

She lost her way again in the lifts. Was she dragged along by the centipede or tottering myriopod pouring from them or sucked in as if by irresistible inward inhalations? Did she perhaps know where she was bound? Dear reader, we can affirm that she didn't. She gasped, floated, swam in a *mare magnum* of plankton like the one described by the professor of paleobiology to a select audience (we don't know to which floor our character has led us astray with so many comings and goings): the one contained in different isotopes of carbon from the metamorphic rocks formed and sedimented on the sea floor, etc. The dame in the horsehair hat listened but didn't hear. A few meters away, a Third-World-looking lad sniffed a glue-soaked handkerchief. What was he doing there among so many doctors and lovers of science? Had he also got the wrong floor, the wrong lecture? Snatches of sentences reached her ears, as if blown on the wind: "microscopic globules of graphite," "clusters of synthetic molecules," "ancient pelagic organisms." My God, what confusion! How could she cram it all in? She suddenly thought that perhaps her hat hindered a correct perception of the scientific discourse: but was afraid to take it off lest the transparency of her skull should bring into view her encephalic mass and its cryptic ramifications. From the evocation of chiasmas, fissures and marrows she proceeded to the nirvana of contemplative specula-tion: witnessed the explosion of gamma rays, the prolegomena to another Big Bang. Was there any way to adapt all that information and data to her peanut-seller, rumbera rhythms? The idea came to her: give science a tune, air it in some gangway choreographed by Béjart and costumed by Valentino. Stage the progress made over the last ten thousand years and relive the big explosion at the edge of the cosmos! Her fragile skiff of thought flipped.

The new person sitting beside her was a lady whose initials "M.P." embroidered on a Chanel suit she had glimpsed when furtively leaf-ing through Father Trennes' manuscript. She was speaking French to a swarthy, pint-sized Andalusian, his parting carefully drawn to hide unsuccessfully his bald pate, and extravagantly garbed like a Napoleonic gent painted by David. Someone whispered in her ear: "It's the libertine Abbot!" Our heroine trembled: how to handle the arrant anachronism?, and was immediately tormented by doubt: rather wasn't she the anachronism? Her anguish spread, covered her like a Breton tide at the June solstice. Where and when had she left her pink soutane? At the masked ball with the gasolines or in the nightly hustle of whores and cars on Prado del Rey?

She slipped from the room after checking her hat was tightly pulled down. More hubble and bubble. People rushing to some Dialogue of Solomons. She saw the Maître des Conférences emerge on a stretcher—shrouded?—laden down with euro-novels. Support, Succor and Hummingbird reappeared in different degrees of muscular, capillary and feathery agitation. They'd found the secret way to the lift to the roof-terrace. Thence they surveyed the restless ocean of the city and its huge range of piscatorial specimens!

They peered out at the top of the Circle and then climbed higher, up a metal ladder, to the top of the dome. Diffused by the haze, the sponge-cake city stretched out of sight. Surprisingly, the anemic sun had halted in its tracks. The dame in the horsehair hat—astute reader, you'll have twigged it by now: she's a transvestite—consulted her wrist watch. Time wasn't flying, everything was in suspense. An angel or airborne creature had lifted off from the top of the Twin Towers and, after a celestial reconnoitre, approached the Gran Vía. Succor and Support anticipated her thought.

The venerable!

Yes, Monsignor!

He came from his Marquis's estates (thank you, Generalíssimo), wearing an Honorable Prelate's cape and a top-rated beatific halo (as the exclusive supplier of all ecclesiastical paraphernalia). He levitated at the Alcalá-Gran Vía crossroads over Minerva's comely bosom. Perhaps he was looking for Friar Bugeo? Our heroine thought it the case. The message he carried promised to be transcendental (her brain fleetingly entertained an idea: should she sign up for a course in transcendental meditation?). How on earth could she have left her video cassette recorder at home? She downed another pill (a cocktail of vitamin B and female hormones).

Then heard the paternal tones of the man accustomed to the commerce of souls.

The thousand less one maxims or amorous sayings fell like confetti over the wreaths and tinsel, in the choir of a plateresque church with Bernini altar-pieces and camp choreography. Background music: a gentle mélange of Gershwin, Sinatra and the Cosa Santa's hymn, bagpipes and percussion. (Support and Succor looked on flabbergasted. Hark, you too, pious reader.)

"Don't step backwards, don't go all soft on me!"

"Go down the paths of prayer and love, seek out volume, weight, relief."

"Grow inwardly!"

(The twin Sisters sighed: what a saintly stroke!)

"There is not one obstacle you won't conquer in your apostolic enterprise . . ."

"Leave a trace!"

"Fortify and hoist aloft the strength of your virtue . . ."

"Take the tabernacles by force!"

"Like bellows that have been constrained, you'll reach further than you have ever dreamed . . ."

Succor: *aquest home és un beneit, un benedetto!* Support: *je suis pénétrée de sa parole!* Succor: I'm gobsmacked! The Paraclete had granted them the gift of tongues.)

"God wants a fistful of men in every human activity . . ."

"Compel, push, pull, deploy your imperious knowledge!"

"Don't let your instruments gather dust!"

(The twin Sisters in tandem: too true! The chubby cherubim on the altar-piece smiled naughtily, knowingly.)

"Don't let your projects be Bengal flares flashing for a moment only to leave charred debris to be cast scornfully aside . . ."

"Be sturdy, surrender yourselves willingly, willfully!"

"Seek out a saint, place yourselves under his protection and feel the strength of his healing powers, his rock-hard faith will soothe your anxieties."

(Support: the all-curing potion! Succor: the infallible recipe! Hummingbird expertly catches a buzzing bluebottle.)

"Carry out the imperative command and . . ."

(Succor, philosophically: the categorical imperative!)

". . . you shall sing like the soul enamored after it has seen the wonders wrought by the Lord . . . Be cogs in his Holiness's great Machine!"

(The cassette came to a halt.)

The final words descended from the void and died there. The beatific halo drooped, then twisted through the air, suddenly banged to the ground. Monsignor no longer levitated over the Minerva on the corner and faded into the background of the frame, towards the Twin Towers. Traffic on the Alcalá-Gran Via crossroads had stopped. The crowd—car and taxi-drivers included—contemplated the wan sky, the pale clouds, the huge, melancholy cardboard scenario where his Worshipful's figure glided and was lost. The traffic cops' spirited whistles made little impact on the snarl-up. Everyone had witnessed the Apparition; but seen differently. Someone was graced by the relic of a holy tear on the slope of their nose. A lady begged for forgiveness amid convulsions bordering on the epileptic. Many unbelievers converted to the creed and several of the faithful lost it. The vicar from the nearby church poured holy water over her. Shouts, whistles, hooters crescendoed into a deafening tumult. Was it auguring in the Apocalypse? Support and Hummingbird read her thoughts through her translucent forehead.

The cycle of transmigration was recommencing!

6   FRIAR BUGEO'S TRANSMIGRATIONS

1

When I reincarnated as someone who must be among those well-balanced friars of which the proverb runs "look at them from afar and speak to them sideways," I did so via the workings of a massive, lengthy cock that visited my mother's grotto until it dripped sperm. I'll not reveal my name or the name of my birthplace, since I intend on hiding the former behind Friar Bugeo's, author of *A Cock-Eyed Comedy* that you, mischievous reader, now grasp between your sweaty palms. As I duly narrated in that work of speculation, written to honor the very ancient prick of the noble and devout Don Diego Fajardo, imitating the lofty style of the most renowned Juan de Mena in his Labyrinth of Fortune, I won't turn over yet again the furrows of his fertile harvest but, by reviewing the glorious deeds and feats of his life, I shall leave a record of the acts I left high and dry when my pen ran away with me. It was I who took his precious relic to the Coliseum in Rome, later transferred by devout, contemplative souls to its present resting-place, in the vicinity of the Villa Tevere. There, the Congregation for Divine Worship and the Sisters of Perpetual Succor evince it daily in their prayers and mental and spiritual exercises.

I grew up in a discordant kingdom, its inhabitants being querulous over questions of honor and lineage. While King Henry rode the land assuaging fires fanned from his saddle with mules and country bumpkins, the cleresy also sought solace along nefast byways. *The Songs of the Provincial* passed from hand to hand, the reading of which much pleasured me before I entered higher orders, during my classes of theology and sod-all in lecture-halls and common quarters:

Ay, friar count without county,
constable without gain,
where's the bounty
in being a famed villain?
"Fucking and being fucked
fornicating round and round,
though my game's sucked,
they'll not keep me bound."

"Provincial, so you may enjoy,
what about this lovely boy?
he's a deep well ready
to cool your vine, and so heady."

Other verse, similarly caustic and sour, fell from my memory like faded leaves enfeebled by the fatigues of old age. Yet I wish to resume the thread of my discourse, that I may relate the famous feats in arms of Don Diego Fajardo, which, with right on my side, I compared to those of the Cid.

Rewarded by his Catholic Majesties with the privilege of selling indulgences to redeem the tribulations of souls in Purgatory, Bulls for the Holy Crusade and other devoutly lucrative commerce, this pious ecclesiastic exhibited from the womb, according to his midwife, all the signs of a horny harrier who'd have topped the desires, were he not victim of Father Time, of Our Lady of the Molls, the best, the perkiest Roman whore that ever came into the world. They tell how though in its prehistory, his mother showed off to her women neighbors his then famous member, tongue spilling from hood. Testimonies to its precocity and proclivities—the latter lauded centuries thence by a Monsignor's inspired quill—were gathered in Acts by his apostles and can be consulted today in the archives of the Fondazione Vaticana Latinitas.

When I met him, he was already a gallant jouster. He would tickle the fancy of any wench, whatever her condition and state, elevating her to heavenly heights with salacious good humor. In wretched times like these when pettiness hides virtue beneath a bushel, it is an act of faith and charity to expound the deserving deeds of my personage before God lowers the curtain on the universe He created because of our manifold sins. This grain of truth should be the needle of the compass that guideth the sick in spirit.

Don Diego also earned income from various concubinages and would often go thence to inspect the honor and care of his wards. His unravellers of first threads and maidenheads, even of the second and third, trawled the realm, like old Celestina, seeking out duennas and Franciscan nuns and he tasted them all, from the first flowerings to the golden glow of the September grape.

One day the fame reached his ears of a lass of very pretty parts, destined by her parents to be a nun in a closed convent. The novice lived in a bedchamber ordered like a chapel where she chastised the rebellious bent of her lusty flesh with fasts and flagellation. Fajardo, very devout and gentle, contrived to see her, asking her sweetly: "Are you a bride of the Lord?"

"Truly I am and will be until the day I die: I shall walk obediently the path of the righteous, for I desire to be by His side in paradise."

"You resolve rightly to flee the world and your insistence is wondrous to all. But it is a thing of reason to taste of it before retreating and turning your back."

"I understand you not, sir."

"Nobody knows the melon's sour, if it's never cleft, and you've not assayed therein."

Thus, with arguments good and persuasive, he revealed a kindly inclination to favor her and a desire to instruct her in the things of the world that she might fulfil all the better her resolve to depart it.

"I am astonished to hear such original words so different to those of my parents and my confessor."

"Better we pass from words to deeds and then you will comprehend me."

And after showing her the size and sturdiness of his member, he quoted from Aristotle and many other sages of Antiquity and touched her and uncovered her body until it was naked, and knelt before the silky, pretty ferns of her grotto, in order to kiss and run his saintly tongue over her lips and cherry whilst he said to her "Blessèd be God, who created such portents and marvels," and a whole anthology of ejaculatories and righteous sayings.

The maiden was stunned by so much novelty and delight, not knowing whether it was the work of Him on high or the devil's.

"All that you do to me, sir, is it not sin of the flesh?"

"To follow nature is not, nor can it be sinful, for it is God-given for our recreation. Lie with me on yonder couch and we shall both ascend to the heavens whither the blessed do eternal dwell."

The unwary maiden obeyed him and Don Diego Fajardo assailed the portico to her vault with caresses and kisses and such was the wisdom of his patter that she consented to open up and welcome in his stave, nay, absorb it right to the hilt. Their prayers and psalms lasted hour after hour, oblivious to the passage of the world and its stars: the aub surprised them both, him a parched plot, her a pot of spume. After this incursion, she who was a novice gleefully surrendered herself to the world, triumphed there and became established as a duenna helped by clergy and nobility. I met her mature and flirtatious, with a retinue of pages and ladies-in-waiting that was the envy of the whole town. I intended having her in my *Cock-Eyed Comedy* but had to pull short, so many and so meritorious were the feats of his eager, horny member.

Before the painful darts of old age confined him to bed and retired his spoke, the stout, antique cock would scatter its seed over the gardens of whores and maidens, Jewish and Moorish, noble and common alike, not pausing to peer pettily at past form and purity of blood. Ace aloft, he'd enter the rooms of his concubines, shake, rattle and roll and not leave one plaintive or angry.

Among the cocky adventures of Don Diego Fajardo, faithful servant to his Catholic Majesties, one deserves a chapter, which occurred in Aragon with an Abbot's secret kept woman, of whom it was said she was a woman of chaste, reclusive ways.

According to the statements some twenty years later by Diego Fajardo to the Holy Inquisition which was persecuting wayward nuns and saintly women, "he did take her hand and pull it toward his thighs bidding her touch a freshly sprung furuncle that had come upon him and she knew he was turned Satan because she felt an object outside his habit and that before that, being one day on her cassock, the aforesaid did place his hands on her breasts and exclaim Oh how holy! Oh how holy!"★

(An addendum gives the word back to the author and a very harsh critique of the man who, at the end of the second millennium, resumed the thread of his Cock-Eyed Comedy, *reincarnated as a self-styled Cosa Santa activist.)*

Such a whippersnapper doesn't know what he's talking about and is a bare-assed liar. I, the real Friar Bugeo, declare and do swear that the valiant, brave-heart cock of Don Diego Fajardo never went in for buttocks but only whores *in fluxu sanguinis* and always sheathed. May he and all his ilk be consumed by the flames of Gehenna that He on High hath prepared for them!

3

To mock and mortify the author of *A Cock-Eyed Comedy* I reincarnated, as he sighed his last, as Seven-on-the-Trot, a Roman pimp of Spanish extraction, friend of Our Lady of the Molls and the whole arm of the Church who paid him their dues in our Soul City.

★ Friar Bugeo attributes to Diego Fajardo the felony of Friar Pedro de Nieva in the convent of Santa Clara in Valladolid (*Amicus Plato, sed magis amica veritas*). (Editor's Note)

From childhood it pleased me much to see lads and even men, mean and lean, and my keen archer's eye knew their worth, what they carried in their breeches for my recreation and the profit of my purse. With the dukes, priors and abbots who summoned me to their quarters to serve at table and pray novenas, I never sold myself short, I haggled and traded in the songs, lilts and tilts of my nation, that are much prized here. If they used me, I used them and, like my grandmammy, milked them to the last drop from their udders, for one thing is to wheel and deal, another our natural longing for a bit of mortar and pestle. I relieved some of money and jewels and others of the sap that stiffens their horns and sticks them where they should deliver. Seeing I was such a little brat, the whores cared for me and procured me Sixto's ointments and aromatic salts, him of the two natures, man as mule and woman as cow, who performed his arts of composition and coupling after retiring through old age and becoming an old curiosity. Thus I ate, drank and prospered, arched my butt and proferred a box to burly, bulky soldiers and grooms.

The Moll and the author of her portrait came to greet me on their promenades and spoke to me of Rome and Spain, of all the works I performed and the tricks of my trade as a mover and shaker.

Moll: The gentleman who describes my feats would like to know from whence you hail and how you learned such a fine, subtle trade. *Seven-on-the-Trot:* I beat it from Cordoba when the Catholic Kings cleansed their kingdoms of the Moors and Jews who were affronting them. And, pardi, it was a very wise and just resolution that brought me to the seat of St. Peter, whose perpetual holiness makes the forbidden licit and hides the wretchedness of the earth under a cloth of bulls and indulgences.

Moll: Poor boy, did you come all by yourself?

Seven-on-the-Trot: With a great aunt harnessed to a Moor for, by all accounts, they tarred and burned my parents in their village.

Moll: Can you read?

Seven-on-the-Trot: Skilled and schooled. I learned my psalms from the Songs of Ropero, Fajardo and other monuments of piety and devotion.

Moll: How did you enter the trade?

Seven-on-the-Trot: My great-aunt says that in my mother's belly I'd already taken a fancy to the mace that visited and off-loaded there.

Moll: Do you get on well with girls on the game? For, upon my faith, many do envy you your tricks of the trade.

Seven-on-the-Trot: We are sisters all and join up and defend ourselves from any out for a free ride! I go to their parties and they come to mine, done up a real treat, a sight for sore eyes. Now and then we mention the ones who mount but don't shoot, the ones who enter the fray and spray wherever they pass; your worship should know we are all devotees of the Madonna and carry her on high to get an airing out of church.

Moll (to her author): None nobler than the sisterhood of whores, because it contains every stock and lineage and clean blood from across the globe: Moors, Jewesses, Gypsies, Illyrians, Corsicans, Lombardans and wenches from Provence and even from northern lands where the sun hides and sickly shines.

Author: Who gave you the name under which you travel?

Seven-on-the-Trot: As the saying goes, a trot pulls more than a rope, and my aunt's spouse's saddle-bag is full of spare 'heads and sponges soaked in hen's blood for marriages and 'head inspections.

Moll (to the author): Devotees of his works never tire of visiting him and he receives and attends to all-comers like St. Michael in his tavern.

Seven-on-the-Trot: The Holy City is a sward of flowers and virtues cultivated lovingly by governors, bishops, humble commoners alike and her tasty fruits are coveted by the saintly men and women in heaven. On High they enjoy their music in the company of angels while down below we relish whatever God and nature gave us, for the members and parts of women and men prefer stroking and fondling to their ordinary usage and this is a source of much wonderment and rejoicing according to the authorized school of philosophers and Ovidians of Antiquity. Or so says the pious Archpriest of Hita and that verse I sing with viola and swinging hips for the noble gentlemen of Rome:

> *For this very deep lake*
> *such greatness contains*
> *it must hold and take*
> *all that meets its domain:*
> *and so I say it is right*
> *for a very good reason*
> *that anything one has*
> *be had by a bigger'un.*

Moll: You are both witty and wise, for it does seem you have suckled doctrine from the breasts of she who gave birth to you.

Seven-on-the-Trot: From the breasts and any hanging garden. Even from those who retire through age I extract their last drop of sap and skin their purse until it's free of ducats. . . .

This was the Rome in which I grew and prospered until that ill-forsaken day when the Constable of Bourbon attacked and sacked it and I put Germans, Franks and Lombards in my sack and they were in a right state, couldn't keep it down. They beat the pan so hard, I was left sick and sore, in pain and beyond cure by incense, resins or ammonia. I putrefied slowly, was a pity to behold, and mirrors frightened me with a sad likeness. Lady Moll beat a timely retreat and went to live with her lover on his island. I ended my days in a dirty, derelict hospital. The Spain that was my first land and punished me newly born also ravaged my cozy cove with blood and fire. Today they call it the watchtower and bastion of the true faith against Luther, Moses and Mahomet. Seeing its deeds and works and all it hath destroyed hither and thither, I tell my innards: better peace in Mecca than the ruination that is Rome.

4

Indifferent to my cruel and undeserved adversity, the wheel of fortune injected me via mouth into the spirit of a famous preacher as he was mounting the pulpit in the Toledan church of San Juan de los Reyes while three hundred leagues away the imperial troops subjugated what was too briefly the merry, carefree capital of Christendom.

Much excited, burning with impatience, I, Friar Francisco Ortiz, awaited the moment to denounce to my flock the crime committed with the very holy bride and soul-sister of Christ, imprisoned in the city a few days prior. The exasperatingly slow march of the clock and the lazy round of the sun fanned my desire to gain a martyr's crown on the cusp of eternal life. In this blind and wretched world that will soon turn dry as hay, in times so full of chaff and bereft of the grain of truth to sustain us, I was driven by the need to bawl out, exclaim and proclaim my faith in that celestial creature, as if it were the last sermon I would give, as if I would perish afterwards, set to suffer every possible torture for the true and good health of my soul.

I spoke, I spewed against those who act like wolves and not shepherds, who deprive the world of the light they do not deserve to behold, who persecute pure, saintly souls, preside over pyres, confiscate property with bastard diligence and cupidity. From on high, as if on a sudden, swirling tide, I surveyed the anguished, disapproving faces of some of the faithful, the restlessness of the brothers in my order, the scornful, contemptuous gestures of those cut to the quick by my massive truth. What else could one expect from men who, attentive only to pomp and circumstance, refute divine illumination with enfeebled argument, dismissing it as illusion and vain fantasy? How could one make prevail over that inquisitorial pack the celestial graces of a most pure virgin whose spiritual, pretty breasts nourished me? Wasn't her girlish, impish innocence and simplicity perchance consubstantial with a supernatural degree of perfection, seraphic wisdom and prudence? God had revealed to her at the age of three the mystery of the Trinity and, with its forgiving sustenance, she had never committed mortal sin. Possessing miraculous gifts of healing through the mere application of one of her garments, with tact and subtlety she helped troubled souls abandon the base and the vile, ate with great difficulty and only after much beseeching, spending days, nay, weeks, without so much as a trickle or doing the necessary.

The clamor surged and the ocean of the world threatened to

engulf my safe haven. I loved her, really loved her, a love pure and clean, averse to carnality and contingency! Her intercession and prayers cured me of the *fluxu seminis* that soiled my nights. Though exempt of all guilt, I lived in perpetual affliction and sadness, in a cruel war against the filth sent forth by the involuntary swelling of my veins. After sundry supplications to God's handmaiden unjustly taken by those who will burn in eternal fire on the Day of Judgement, she set me free from these woeful, abject sores and stains with a strap she girt to my back, and forthwith I witnessed her rise above the earth, close to me, wonderfully beautiful, her tender, benign eyes looking down upon me, as if to say she was watching over me!

The tidal wave of aberrations and angry voices submerged the flow from my lips—"rascal jude" and other insults thrown at my lineage—but they worried me as much as the leaves rustling in the trees. The chains they tried to lock on me I held more precious than a hundred thousand richly bejewelled crowns: I was desperate to be wood for the pyre, to be tarred, pitched and burnt, to see myself reduced to smoke and ashes, freed from the mire and venality of corrupt nature, ascending to the heavens to be at one with my most saintly, illustrious spouse.

The unruly tumult of Christians congregated in the temple did not abate my spirits. Were they fallacious or real those faces, hate-filled and blind to evidence, which would later accuse me of stubborn, Luciferine pride? The brothers in my order had climbed into the pulpit and struggled to silence me, dazzled by the intensity of light, a reflection from the divine sun, emanating from the pretty, petite body of my beloved. Those who labeled her a miracle-working holy woman and victim of libidinous turns wrote off her devotees as damaged heretical goods, mistook the gift of divine grace for the shadow of appearances! Was I trying to pose as a prophet as my enemies later argued? I believe and still believe that I was not. Perhaps the freshness from so much blessed joy deceived my sinful, mortal eyes but, how could it have been otherwise? The incandescence of God's innocent handmaiden lit my candle: her delicious, carnal casing was cool balsam to the ardors of my racing heart. May he who has yet to succumb to the traps and snares of the world cast the first stone!

They wrenched me roughly from the pulpit and dragged me to the Inquisitional prison. There I lived a thousand deaths and saw myself accused of innumerable erroneous, heretical and scandalous propositions worthy of Beghards and Beguins as they stacked up the proof destined to undermine my faith in the virtue of my saint. Finally, I weakened, collapsed, retracted. The devil had deceived me. I accepted my punishment, totally acquiesced and remained cloistered, safe from the horrors and wiles of the created universe, until God took pity on my plight and put a happy end to my days.

(My soul transmigrated from the convent of the Mother of God in Torrelaguna after residing there fifteen years without ever going outside its walls. I despised the world as deeply and bitterly as it had despised me. Centuries later Ángela Selke rescued me from oblivion.)

5

The gentle gossipy breeze about what was happening in the convents swiftly spiralled into a whirlwind. The inquisitors came well rehearsed to cleanse them, thanks to testimonies and confidences gathered therein, not only from friars as pure as the driven snow but also from new Christians worried by the rash lunacy of their blood brothers.

The chain of transmission of such tell-tales spread far and wide and relied on such solid bases as "Priest Tom told me brother Dick had told him that he'd heard that a friar had said he knew who the Harry was who'd told him so from what he'd read on the lips of brother Wilfred" according to the worthy model of the historical chronicles and founding legends of our Mother Spain, that scourge of heretics and beloved in Christ.

Denounciations, strange and harmful statements accumulated in the reports of the most saintly inquisitors who delved into our lives with admirable diligence: one witness related how once when taking recreation with other monks on a river bank, a friar from his convent crouched down, girded up his skirts, thus uncovering his circumcised member and when he reproached him for so doing, the other retorted that "he was born thus" (in like vein do abound more rude, jocular versions whose telling here modesty precludes); another maintained that priest so-and-so didn't configure the cross with his thumbs when joining his hands together in the Introit and grimaced when he said mass and made contemptuous bodily movements and when consuming the wafer, which he called tart, he did so as if communicating with a gross fellow, in a nutshell, as a person who neither believed nor had faith in the Holy Sacrament. Likewise, when the priest raised the body of our Lord, many monks looked at the ground and quietly hummed heresies from their venomous sect.

While to the sound of tambourines cart after cart of wood passed by to feed the pyres of the Holy Office, another convent was in a stew after the discovery of a manuscript by a monk who cast doubt on the virginity of Mary, impregnated according to him "by ear, through the working of the Holy Spirit" who then prayed audaciously: *Mundum aeternum dicimus ab initio, verbo creatum negamus, quod ex nihilo nihil sit, sed cum quad fit ex materia perlatente producitur.* The logs destined to burn in public ceremonies were already stacked around the stakes.

What could one expect of a country whose ideal woman was the manly woman incarnated in her very Catholic and Benign Queen and the love of those of my species for males chastised by the rack, *autos-da-fe* and eternal damnation? The dilemma that gripped us granted no escape route to those born in poor or impure cradles. We had to be virile, but chaste to avoid turning soft or effeminate! To console ourselves we recited the inflamed verse to the Beloved by St. John of the Cross and Mother Teresa: nobody dared commit them to paper for fear of the snoopers who proliferated on the air like hungry flies. The daring declaration of St. John of Ávila also did the rounds: "Those condemned by the Inquisition are martyrs of fanaticism." Yet neither I nor my peers wanted to be martyrs: the anxiety that corroded us didn't allow a moment's respite, incited temerity.

(We hated the curse of chastity and mocked it in our conventicules, disguised in female garments, with castanets, raucous songs and tumultuous clapping.

Arching her buttocks, a novice in a pink soutane danced a zapateado with a fake phallus and a repeated refrain

One friar said to another:
dance or you're a fairy, brother!

until she dropped from exhaustion.)

Green with envy, we listened to tales of Spanish Muslims, adventurers and captives in lands of the Turk. There they all enjoyed untrammelled freedom: the women of the harem fondled and pleasured themselves or had recourse to the arts of skilled eunuchs; fans of the rear eye served the lustiest janissaries and were served by them. The description of Captain Bronzen and other roughnecks glistening with oil, all rippling muscle and broad shoulders, plunged us into a world that was more beautiful, more rugged, far from the evil begrudgers of our mean-spirited territories. The portrayal of bulging arms and pectorals, the wild blaze in their eyes, fanned the flame and magnetic pull of a forbidden delight. As if tightly gripped by pincers, the *morisco* went on, they tested each other's mettle, dragged each other back and forth, round and round like bulls spurred on by awesome jealousy. But that paradise of light and ocular joy was forbidden: our dreams of evasion disappeared in smoke, illusory and chimerical.

Ever since the harassment begun the previous century, we all lived on the alert. The Carmelite arrest of Friar John of the Cross in his cottage of the Incarnation and his secret removal to a high-walled convent on the right bank of the Tagus had spread panic. Nobody, but nobody, was safe from the tight-knit web of snoopers. Some of us were suspected of heresy, others of sodomy or Beghardy, others of stubborn resistance to the most holy custodians of our Credo. We lived in the cruelest times, so much so that I couldn't say which was the more dangerous, to speak or to be silent, thus wrote Erasmus's favorite correspondent. The presence of spies in university halls and chairs silenced any attempt at reflection. God's ministers read our thoughts and desires, however hidden, and we were forced to confess to them under torture.

I well remember the day when a prior, an active disseminator of his seed among the lasses of Castile and Aragon, brought me a battered copy of the *Song Book* which contained the work of Friar Bugeo — with whom I was at one in a previous transmigration — so I could take it to Headquarters and put it in safe-keeping. If it were discovered, he told me, it would land him in more trouble than the Dean of Cadiz with his collection of Arab erotica because there was no room for the felicities of the flesh in realms dedicated to the castigation of the senses and the exaltation of Lady Lent: three Beghard monks and a saintly healing woman had just been burnt in the main square of his town!

And so I spent most of the time incarcerated in my bedchamber with a Philippine flunkey with whom I communicated by signs, and dared not venture out except in the pitch of night. We would go visit the Greek Demeter who, wrongly accused of Islamic ablutions, had suffered a year's imprisonment in a dungeon and, after emerging whitewashed from that test, he lived poorly in a room off a yard frequented by petty crooks: my flunkey and I would slip in there to assuage our ardors with some Moorish slave or galley-hoodlum while the very rude, ruddy-faced prior and other conveniently covered priests relieved theirs on lusty, well-disposed wenches. We had to oil the wheels of the machine so the men of the Holy Office shut their eyes or turned a blind one. Behind its mask of righteous virtue, Spain was an auction-house: everything had its price and the gentlemen inquisitors and their henchmen gorged like leeches.

Centuries after my death, when I roamed the constellations in search of a new transmigration, I read the fictional version of my visit to Friar John of the Cross in his Toledan prison: I don't know if that's how things panned out—the years don't pass in vain—or whether I evoked these memories in a peculiar interdisciplinary congress of Saint Johnnies in a cardboard cut-out spa on the shores of the Black Sea. The dates merge in my memory, people and objects fade and disappear, facts and acts perhaps correspond to different epochs and diverse incarnations, only the Fatherland where destiny condemned me to be born remained unchanging as time rolled on: lethargic minds, threadbare lives, austere landscapes, petrified towns, aeolic erosions. That is how Faustino Sarmiento saw it and so did I as I flew and hovered over the French invasion and civil wars, when accumulated hatred and frenzy were let loose and, in the name of God, King and the Fatherland, they set in motion the machinery of the waterwheel and buckets went down the well empty, to resurface with blood, yet more blood.

They say the Inquisition was abolished but, don't you think it might survive, deep down in our heads?

6

My new transmigration was as cruel in manner as it was unexpected. I wasn't fired straight from the gun-carriage into the uterus but created with a flourish of the pen within the pages of a manuscript which threaded me seamlessly from cradle to grave: not a being of flesh and bone as in previous incarnations, but a hero or rather, anti-hero, pure entelechy. The story concluded, my author returned me to the void, didn't even grant me the great good fortune of survival on the pages of his new conjectures. He thus spared me my sentence to the galleys but, like the Jupiter or God he loathed, he showed me how his writing was as barbarous and crazy as the Fiat that engendered the factory of this universe: the botch-up or sponge cake that is the Creation.

With that same arbitrariness and disdain which rules the engine of the world, he allotted me an impure lineage, made me an object of contempt for the hostile rabble, complete with *sambenito* hanging from the ceiling of the Cathedral. Nor did he grant me the blessing of a birth in a rich cradle—moneys buy nobility and gentrified accoutrements—so I might ride in high society and display great finery; since man has no greater good sense or science than to have and to have yet more. Deprived of all that furnishes lives and estates, from infancy I had to bear my own ball and chain and whomsoever I did wish to flatter in order to ingratiate their good will, would hurl me to the knacker or hold me at arm's length like a leper.

After consulting my pillow, I changed name, birthplace and lineage hoping I'd give spies the slip and be known as Don Guzmán de Alfarache. Though no blockhead, I had ground to cover and strove to become a man of letters and courtly ways, acting up my blue blood, mocking those whose blood had turned thin on them. I was still a lad but, with my gentlemanly airs and and graces, I resolved yet to leave the thousand-times-blessed Spain and seek out better, more pristine ancestors. The reader is acquainted with the upsets and trials of my journey. My maker didn't spare me from any, but battered me like the north wind, lurching me from good fortune to tribulation, landing on my feet, then flat on my face. He turned the page and left me truly in it, on the lines of that proverb "a knife in the guts is the world's best surgeon." Once bleary and bedraggled—necessity has a heretic face—I became bright-eyed and bushy-tailed by the side of the ragamuffins and good-for-nothings I frigged against: one moment riding on embroidered blankets, the next as bare as a fig-tree in winter, one day with pots of dosh, the next out in the moonlight, between pimps and pricks who cared not a hoot for my honor and misused their muscle. The lad who fled those plotters, lineage-watchers and spinners of suspicions found himself repudiated by his Genoan family, converted into an object of their mocking and contempt. Squirreling it as best I could, slinging my kettledrums over my shoulder, I headed for Rome, the Eternal City, seat of our Holy, Infallible Mother. I was a bright idea barely touching the ground. Upon my arrival, I suffered an onset of tears of joy: rushed to embrace her holy ramparts, kissed her holy soil.

My leg laid low by scrapes and japes I prefer to pass on, I planted myself before the portals of a cardinal by no means partial to plonkers and famed for his piety who, as he left his sacred palace, stopped to harken unto me: Alms, noble Christian, have pity on this sinner laid low by an affliction of his limp limbs! Behold the sad state of my years! Oh, most Reverend Father, most Illustrious Monsignor!

After listening carefully and going straight to the kernel of my tribulation with wondrous illumination, Monsignor did take extreme pity on me. He did order his servants to carry me in their arms into his house and relieve me of my ragged, worn-out apparel, wash me and then place me on his bed after placing his own in the adjacent chamber.

O God who art so great and good! O what largesse from that gentlemanly estate! They did strip and dress me, spare me from begging in order to give unto me, so I could give unto others. God only taketh away, so He can shower more bountifully. This hallowed male followed in his imitation. After informing himself that

I was clean and tidy, Monsignor perkily approached my quarters. He warmed to the sight of me because my figure, face and fruits were a perfect fit. Expertly, like a saint practiced at what he performs, he stooped to peruse my peter and caressed it with silken hands. Stroking, fingering, invoking the Madonna, whom he worshipped devoutly, he concluded his task with a great spurt of thanksgiving straight from the heart.

"Lord and Master of all that we survey," did he say. "One tailor's needle never leaves another's idle!"

I'll drop it there because exercises in holiness are the water of life, a blessed bread and joy fit for angels. 'Twas all a present from God as were the graces and favors that rained upon me. My author didn't labor the point so as not to become wood for the bonfire and, though the oversight of our holy guardians granted him the *nihil obstat*, he was forced to put the deep blue sea between himself and them and hasten to New Spain with only what he stood up in.

Monsignor tenderly loved those who served him, putting them second only to his love for God. He wanted my good repair so dearly as if his own did depend thereon; and to test out whether he could win me to acts of virtue, he played at tease and take, removed any opportunity or desire for me to spread myself elsewhere. When he was eating tidbits, he'd partake with me: "Ducky little Guzmán, with this I give thee a truce, I sign a pact of peace. Savor this mouthful and stay a likely lad, for the banquet's nigh."

He would beam all over his face, worrying not a jot about the nobles and gentlemen at his table. He was most humane and courteous, engaged and esteemed his servants, cherished them, loved them, did everything possible for them, so they loved him from the bottom of their souls, and most faithfully: for, without a doubt, the servant serves the master who well respects him, and well paid is he who pays well. So I wasn't left alone, a prey to temptations from the fancily decked, rude-tongued women parading by night beneath our windows, he did lay in my bed and bestow upon me prayers and blessings from his breviary.

The other pages' envy of my state of grace combined falsehood and unfairness against me. Their aspersions as to my larceny uncovered my evil, thieving inclinations capable of losing all for nothing and mongered rumors about my night-bird flights and sallies. Seeing me one day in only petticoats and flounces, Monsignor, face overcast, dismissed me from his service in order to put me to the test: however much his heart was riven, however many messengers he despatched, testimony to his love for me and his suffering at my absence, I acted as deaf as a post and only harkened to my choler: I did act basely and did stay base and ungrateful towards God's good grace and favors that reached me via the hands of that hallowed, masterful male. How disloyal to the charity which I was dealt! How blind to his wit and good works! Monsignor's multiple mischievery manifested his real condition, inherited from the true Father, to do good and even better to such as I.

And so I returned to my life in the wild, knapsack on back, though I vied to retrieve embers with a cat's paw and unrolled more coils than any octopus, my devious intent did lead me astray in fresh scrapes and associations. Better to be ignorant as a yoked heifer than a donkey burdened by science!: the pretense that I was who I wasn't caught me out and dropped my bones behind bars in the hospital where paupers and the bankrupt tumble pell-mell.

The writer did deal right rigorously with my arrogant determination. In order to punish me with a cuckoo's call, after marrying me to the jingle of bells, he upgraded me to go-between and had me sell above the counter what hasn't or should not have a price: it was said without filigree or finery that with my wife I did bring peace to a rich governor and he would bring me as a real Adonis, sleek and sweet-smelling, for being so attentive to his desires.

Grief struck me seeing my first fluff and whiskers and then at so quickly them frotting freely elsewhere: and as is the lot of jesting pages and those privy to ministers of Venus and Cupid, the more trouble others took to settle and season me, the greater grew their disdain for my commerce. But as everything on our stage is a double-edged dagger, I worried not a whit at having my customs slighted or at getting mud in the mocker.

My creator pursued my frenzied life from arse to tit, and ever downhill. I stole, I plied, I traded my wife's box of tricks, I gambled, grievously bodily harmed, was banged up, sentenced to the gallows. Though I soon climbed into the confidence of the overseer, because I was equal to his every desire, and though with the love he professed me he didn't inflict harsh servitude to the oar, my horns far from the hunt stoked jeering malevolence: my shame-faced lineage and winsome ways were the most common tittle-tattle.

But to tell the truth what really fed my fear and distress was the precipitate chase of the printed page: I could see the distance shorten separating me from the end to the Second Part of my life, with no great expectations that my creator would commit to a Third. How could I rebel against a destiny drawn from such harmonious spheres? My hatred for the writer and those pleasured by a reading of my misfortunes was as virulent as the venom he directed towards the Maker of the great factory of the universe. Like Jupiter—let's dub him so for the sake of simple self-preservation—

overjoyed, or so they say, to see the beauty of the orb with its stars and constellations, he worked himself hard, with the sagacity and immense bookishness of those who pride themselves on being learned, winding up the novel not pausing to think that he thus delivered me to the nothingness whence I emerged at the start; and, like the donkey created before Adam, I burned to whinny and buck and dirty the book with a shower of what it had coming, leaving the space of the discourse where he slotted me in the filth and the mire. That should be my parting shot and not the cruel sentences with which he terminates the final chapter.

My cruel inventor had told me in advance through the two Parts of the work: "from Adam to myself many have come and gone but none has lived out the century." My existence as Guzmán was even shorter-lived. He did last a few more years of hurly-burly and saved his skin and bones from the pyre. I was stitched up well and good, and without hope: my rosary of misfortunes rounded off with a derisory *Laus Deo*.

As proof of the calamity and catastrophe of the Creation, the ears and noses of many Moors hung from the galley's mast. My author did brook no pity for them either.

7

A surprise so divine!

As my soul expanded and lodged in mortal flesh I discovered in the mirror my lack of the little bundle with which I usually reincarnated: instead of the fatuous excrescence from previous transmigrations, I had a smiling set of labials and a diminutive nacreous button whose perfections left me in ecstasy.

That beauteous, compact wonder proclaimed my pure virginal condition and I resolved to remain so until the end of my days, and never sully myself on a male. From when I left the tit and began to enter the realm of reason, I stayed hours and hours absorbed before that singular novelty, seeking to derive strength from frailty and defend myself against mundane assault. Thus I memorized all the prayers in the *Book of Saints* and a great abundance of pithy Latin mottoes. I pretended to muse and immerse myself in deep meditation over the blessed souls in Purgatory and the mysteries of the Trinity. I enjoyed the astonished admiration of adults, delighted to hear myself called a saint. Though it was not my good fortune to be born in a media century, I performed like a professional artiste in the spotlight, confronted the quizzical eyes of press and cameras. Emulating angels and other celestial creatures, I fed exclusively on flowers and the pearly dew that drenched them. My house filled with money, offerings and ex-votos, like the chapel of Christ in Agony in the great cathedral.

I had seen a beautiful, luminous, translucent Lady levitate before me and gaze upon me most benignly. The Gentlewoman rejoiced in the vision of my little garden and sweetly offered a garland of roses to gird my waist as a garment of perpetual chastity.

"God wants you intact for Himself and commends that you transmit His words to the world. Much evil will descend upon the Earth if men give themselves over to the vice of luxury. There shall be wars, earthquakes, plagues, whirlwinds and other foul indication of death and desolation. Tell the faithful to pray and fast, that God is angry with them and, the more complacent they feel, the quicker will descend his punishment."

The day I recited the *summas* of Thomas of Aquinas, when I cured two sickly people with my ribbons and levitated above the garden in a golden halo, my fame spread far and wide. I was pleased to shut myself in my chambers before my full-length mirror and while tens, nay hundreds, of devotees moaned outside, genuflecting and beating their breasts, I examined my little cherry and pretty nacreous shell, infatuated with its purity of line, caressing them with the tips of my fingers until I moistened in love. How I scorned the rough, brutal ways of men and the vile act with which they procreated! Their brusque manners and heavy breathing (I knew my progenitors!) caused me to vomit. My universe was a meadow of pretty little girls, indulging in naked water-games with the cheerful candor of childhood. The Lord and His Divine Intercessor, smiling down from on high, exhorted me to keep pure, helped by my Guardian Angel and a flock of wingèd seraphim.

As triumph led to triumph and the number of my devotees multiplied, I appeared before them more frequently with the stigmatas of the Cross or levitated over the richer, ever more abundant offerings placed on my doorstep. Neither Bernadette Soubirou nor the swain of Fatima enjoyed as much glory as I. I never involved myself in politics like them, or condemned atheistic communism, but trained my revelations on the workings of sex. I affirmed that the carnal act, even between people united by holy matrimony, offended the gaze of the celestial powers-that-be: angels covered their eyes to avoid seeing, it gave the Virgin the willies and Boy Paul the Saint torture more cruel than whatever his Roman executioners could inflict. "They behold all you do," I told them, "and though you do it in the dark, they abhor your incontinence. We women are born intact and should die intact. Procreation is a ploy of the devil."

There was discord and controversy. Some believed the truth of my dicta and others put me down as a snotty little girl and whiner. The inquisitors sent their spies to watch over me and inspect my food and waters, to count the exact number of my prayers and incantations. Then, someone swore under oath he'd seen me play with another girl's pretty little cherry and show great signs of contentment. They tried to catch me and take me caged to the most famous exorcist in the diocesis, but I beat them to it: I levitated, flew and flew far from the peninsula. I initiated a new life in the seraglio of the Great Turk. Protected from the world by the inviolability of the harem, until the day I died I enjoyed the company of other women, was served and entertained by eunuchs. And so it was that I fulfilled my desires and those of Our Lord God and Master.

9

I was the first forebear of Tristram Shandy, Blas Cubas and Christopher-the-Unborn, although unlike three-in-one I didn't conclude my literary life at the door to the maternal cloister and couldn't dialogue with the reader-selector through its multiple veils.

My parents would chatter about their lack of heirs until one day when my mother wasn't thinking, I sicked up at her stomach-gates. She truly feared my coming as she'd not received her usual letters: three months without a missive from me. As my volume increased, she waxed anxious and argued with her husband over my sex. She wanted a girl, unaware of the little bundle already poking up from my lower midriff.

"Sinner woman," he retorted, "can't you see a daughter generates nothing and that a boy does?"

"I know," said she, "that a daughter cannot lift what a boy can, but perhaps one woman has stirred lots of men from seed scattered o'er the earth and strung them from the horns of the moon."

Gradually, as the days passed and my limbs and bodily possibilities formed and strengthened, I realized what a dangerous funnel my birth would be: reaching out for life to meet but death. As history teaches, ever since the world was the world, the swaddling clothes of today are the shrouds of tomorrow. From cradle to grave, from first whimper to last croak the measure of time is infinitesimal compared with the Lord's after his capricious coining of Adam. Terrified by this savage law, I resolved to cling to the rocks and parapets of my protective grotto and not breathe air. I learned the lessons of life without moving from my cozy cave. Knowledge of the world's brutal inequalities, of abuse wrought by lords, the misery of vassals, the plague of snoopers, theft by ministers reinforced my resolve to resist nature and the repetition of its cycles. I surmised from my parents and their conversations with their neighbors that we lived in a decrepit country on course to ruination: a republic which devoured its children, an irremediably barren waste, both prison to the intellect and dungeon to the senses. After nine months of fortunate enclosure, could I allow myself to be pitched into a much more somber jail? What was the universe if not a cornucopia of empty pretense, fantastic genealogies, petty progress and sleight-of-hand, a stage or arena of false pieties destined to conceal a furious thirsting after power and money? Were those who stalked night and day registering actions, noting demeanors, looking into eyes, scrutinizing ideas, libelling lips going to indulge my desire to live unfettered or think on my own account? What turbid decision engendered me, merely to hurl me down such a vile precipice?

I dreamed of Tristram and Uncle Toby, of the Brazilian excursions of Blas Cubas and forged an inner dialogue with Christopher-the-Unborn, creating chimerical genealogies for myself but able to link the sorry decline of Hapsburg Castile to the cheerful beaches of Acapulco where on that 12 October 1992, an ill-fated day for Spanishry and the braggadocio of the Fifth Centenary, the lad would see the light of day. My every lunatic fantasy converged on another orb, alien to my inventor's and his sad destiny: to change state and leave his fatherland, to return clandestinely, be betrayed by spies and die in a very secret prison.

The laughter I heard from the belly tasted tearful. Why did they mercilessly force me into this century knowing full well what it held for me? Did the foolish, insipid Gregorio Guadaña, unmetamorphosed by the work of a genius like Gregor Samsa, really deserve the trials and tribulations of a childhood that in the end would serve no end? If only my inventor had left me on the first pages of his manuscript after breaking his quill or running out of ink! Then could I have enjoyed a happy fetal existence, rocked by the sound of waters, instead of embarking on a countdown to a life of hard knocks in a Spain of deluded men, hostile to all productive activity and free exercise of thought likely to trouble their peace of mind and becalmed habits. None of that happened and I shriveled in a pool of spilt ink, cursing my stubborn, aggrieved scribe and the obstinacy of He who, out of a desire for fame, fashioned the absurd, shiny engine that is the world.

I didn't attain the posthumous glory of a Tristram or Blas Cubas or Christopher-the-Unborn: I stuck on Gregorio Guadaña, went from nothing to nothingness.

10

I wandered the skies lost in the immense void populated by stars and meteorites, trying to divine the signs of the Zodiac and which was mine. I remembered the gentle words of Empedocles of Agrigento: "I have been a boy, a girl, a plant, a bird, a silent fish leaping from the sea," but didn't succeed in casting out my sad condition as a rational being and persisted in my transmigrations, condemned harshly to change my carnal covering and bid farewell to the century.

When I breathed my last sigh from the mouth of Gregorio Guadaña I decided to consult a soul-mate of Friar Bugeo who had seen off dozens of bodies without ever settling for one.

(She had been a haltered black slave, kept Indian of a conquistador, tavern hussy, cuckold with deer's antlers, lusty serving wench in an inn, Franciscan tertiary, bishop *in partibus*, privy to the king, prior's concubine, fugitive from the Inquisition, youth of pleasant parts and puny brain.)

"So much roaming the gloaming to fall into the same trap!"

(She consoled herself, she told me, by reading Gracián and Latin poets and prose writers.)

"Who decides our fate so capriciously?"

"Christen him Jupiter or the Goddess Fortune for in times like these it would be rash to call him by his name."

(My desire for knowledge displeased her and she fidgeted to demonstrate her disgust.)

"Tell me, if you know, what law governs the created world and the rational creatures inhabiting it?"

"The pleasures of the flesh and money," said she. "The rest is *galimatias* concocted to breed feelings of guilt among the congrega-

tion and reinforce the dominion of those who abrogate the power
to rule the flock in the first place!"

(I saw her take flight, disappear amid the clouds, show no sign
of compassion.)

Abandoned to my meandering, I was woman and man, grandee of
Spain and beggar, mender of maidenheads and midwife of much
insight and foreplay
danced like a jolly frog for stuffy nobles and instructed in vain
dumb bachelors, incarnated as a damsel and turned handsome gallant on behalf of the girl I loved (discovered chit-chat was super-
fluous, that the tongue had better uses and abuses)
when Pythagoras's rooster sang I dawned as an overseer with singed
mustache and sunk my aft into the youngest galley-slaves and hours
later woke up eight months pregnant wanting to spew up the lin-
ings of my soul

I imagined I was God at the dawn of Creation, at the moment
the sun pitilessly illumines the world and reveals the irrevocable
magnitude of the Disaster
    wars, persecutions, tyrannies, famine, dogmatic,
oppressive religions, women enslaved, doctrinal
aberrations, Conciliar hypocrisy, ecclesiatical celibacy, divine
versus natural law, punishment of the flesh, stoning of
adulteresses, burning of the nefast

From body to body, an endless meandering and pilgrimage, I
discovered the vain pomposity of nobles, the dire straits of gentlemen, the impoverished state of the people, the discrediting of work

and commerce, the bile of the erudite, the vast felonies of ministers, the stupid profligacy of monarchs

I enjoyed my mother's warm milk, semen poured in my open
jaws, the inner melting away of cavities visited by tongues and fingers, all manner of drinks, wines and dishes

I touched, stroked, caressed tits and pricks, opulent butts, rear
half-moons, shadowy nooks, deliciously damp caves, stalactites and
fastnesses

Suddenly, as if in a dazzling theophany, I espied Friar Bugeo
wrapped in the spiritual halo of his Archimandrite's cloak. He
found me, he said, sad and moping, undesirous of prolonging my
temporal existence.

"You mustn't lose heart," he counseled. "It's been like this from
the beginning of the Reconquest. Carnal sin is the devil at work to
soften and womanize us. Haven't you heard the tale of Pelayo, that
most beautiful ephebe, who preferred torture and death to yielding
to the torpid desires of Caliph Abdelrahman? For centuries our
compatriots have identified forbidden pleasure with their mortal
enemies. Every medieval chronicle harps on this theme."

"Wouldn't it be better for me to be born a woman and enjoy
my parts like our Lady of the Molls?"

"God spare you such a puerile pensée! Women have been and
are the cause of the soul's perdition. On a visit to Rome with other
leaders of the Cosa Santa, Monsignor admonished his sons come
from every confine of the world, and lay before us the exemplary
heroism of sweet (naturally unaware of the adjective's connotations

on Arabic tongues) San Bernardo who, to ward off the woman who climbed into his bed with lascivious intent as *procax meretrix cum palpabat*, remained immune to her caresses following the *fugite fornicationem* legislated by numerous Councils of the Church."

"What must I do then, Reverend Father? Be a manly woman? A chaste, bored man? Neither option tempts me. Am I condemned to be reborn only to suffer persecution once more?"

"Let not the fire of love be a firefly! All that's done in the name of love gains substance and uplifts. Listen to Monsignor: 'You and I will give and be given with no half-measures.'"

(Our souls dallied in the heavens near cirrus and stratus clouds where, according to the ubiquitous, anachronistic Father Trennes, Pelayo the martyrized infant used to linger.)

"He's not half gone rotten on me! (he smiled). Now he spends his whole time looking for pick-ups, the sure spigot of some Straightshooter the Saint of Barbès loves so much. But there are no archers or artillery corporals here. I knocked into him the other day and rebuked him affectionately but firmly with these our Founder's words: 'Leave those childish, effeminate poutings and flouncings! Be a man!'"

"Wouldn't a sex-change suit him better?"

"By now you ought to know how light-heeled and inclined to vice women are. Characters soft and sweet like meringues offend Monsignor. I've found his maxims invaluable. Thanks to them, I've pledged my life to the pursuit and conquest of real saints."

(Father Trennes wrapped round his elegant cloak, ready to take flight and disappear into the immensity of space.)

"Please, don't leave me!" I shouted.

"I've a religious date in the Luxor and don't want Saint Juan of

Barbès to beat me to it. The cream of my canonized brethren awaits me!"

Ignoring my entreaties, with characteristic selfishness, he abandoned me to my destiny, a veritable waterfall of tears.

Weary of so much barbarism and repetition, I tried to bid farewell to the cycles of the sun and enigmas of the universe, to be fodder for worms and dust of this earth, but I went unheeded and the water-wheel, its buckets laden with bodies wasted, then constantly renewed, went on and on turning.

I then crossed a void of much more than half a century and reappeared in Barcelona in the shadow of Father Trennes disguised as the Philippine flunkey who saw to his flat in San Gervasio: it was the time he was on intimate terms with Gil de Biedma and friends, as recorded at the beginning of this book. I was renowned for being shy and reserved, but soon put a stop to that. I let my hair down and flew off with a fine flock of gaudy fairies.

7 FROM SEX WITH THE ENLIGHTENED TO SEX WITH THE SIXTY-EIGHTERS

Of course I was aware of what Deep Purple Don Marcelino says in the chapter which he devotes to me with characteristic Christian generosity: a bitter, shambolic polemicist, an incredulous materialist, a spreader of sophistry, a kicker against all the pricks, a hater of all middle ways and restrictions on thought, an opponent of any kind of yoke . . . But what I really found irritating was his attempted pen portrait: he depicts me as someone "very, very small, dark-skinned, horribly ugly, more like a satyr from the forest than a human being" and goes on to add, "despite that and his poverty he thought all women loved him, which made him the butt of most hilarious pranks not suitable for a serious work of this kind." I immediately went and posed for the photographer on the boulevard Saint Martin for a full-length picture and sent it to his abode at the Academy of History with a sarcastic one-liner: Look at yourself in the mirror, Deep Purple! I don't know whether he received it because I never got a reply.

That I was loved by a large of number of women can be confirmed by those implicated: my friend M.P., to whom Father

Trennes refers in his *Lives of Saintly Men* proclaims to the heavens that I always served and delivered to such a degree that she placed me at the head of the top scorers in her love league of more than five hundred gallants: the proof of love is in the pudding, not in good intentions!, which she translated as *il n'y a que les faits de plumard qui comptent!*

One cannot object to the withering critique of my philosophical and political ideas. Deep Purple embodies the clerical obscurantism I most detest and it is only logical and natural he vituperates against them. There are honors that slander and slanders that honor. To tell the truth, the crude aggression meted against me made me proud. I was in fact thinking about that the day I bumped into Friar Bugeo—a heteronym of Father Trennes, whose life and miracles the reader is familiar with—near his *appartement* on the Right Bank. His Sixties revolutionary fervor had deserted him after a trip to the USSR and he attended with saintly alacrity to other, more substantial tasks on the boulevard Rochechouart and in the lavatories of the Gare du Nord. He'd not showed up for some time at our gatherings of exiles from the different Spanish civil wars of the last two centuries, apparently absorbed in his apostolic endeavors.

"I had just sent my photo, in a smart suit and tie, to my first author (I call him that because they are legion who write on these matters): the physical portrait he pens of me is a grotesque he. How about meeting for a coffee and chinwag?"

"Better if you come to my place. I can treat you to an excellent Bordeaux from this year's harvest. According to the enologists it's the best there's been for fifteen years, although I don't know if it's as good as the one your admired predecessor and master sent to

Voltaire: *et je bois les bons vins dont Monsieur d'Aranda vient de garnir ma table*, if you remember?"

I followed him to his rooms and settled down on the sofa of his three-piece which, like the rest of the furniture, was exactly the same as in the Barcelona flat described in the first chapter of this book. Friar Bugeo switched on the sitting-room lights and, while he was going to the kitchen in search of the precious bottle, I amused myself by taking a peep at the distinguished rows of antique-bound volumes in his library. Deep Purple's *The History of Spanish Heterodoxy* in a luxury edition, lauded it on one of the middle shelves. Friar Bugeo uncorked the Bordeaux and poured the wine with the savoir-faire of a maître d'hôtel.

"What about yourself?"

"For some time I've been on water only."

"Have you made a promise to the Virgin or to the Holy Guardian Angels?"

"No. I'm simply trying not to make a fool of myself."

He looked at me: his features had gone flabby and hardly recalled those of Father Trennes. I was about to say as much, but he rushed in first.

"Yes, Deep Purple's diatribes are excessive at times. The ideas of each epoch directly influence us and in the century when you were brought up these were the ideas of the Enlightenment and the Encyclopedia. Rousseau literally believed his doctrines would redeem the world, never imagined the horrors of the Revolution and the Terror. You, my dear libertine abbot, and those school textbooks dub as Frenchified, were somewhat ingenuous. History punishes the naive and any who step out of line: whether in the Napoleonic invasion or the recent democratic transition. The people who benefit from the changes are those who advance their pawns at the right moment. You should read the manuals of Guizot and Paul Preston more carefully."

"Despite your present disillusion and elegant cynicism, you also thought Communism would spread seeds which would germinate and produce happiness for humankind.

You travelled to Cuba and came back trumpeting the wonders of the Revolution and its leaders at the very moment they were crushing the freedoms they had preached and were submitting their people to a political inquisition worthy of the Jacobins. Why didn't you retract then? I did and fulminated against Robespierre, Marat and *L'ami du peuple*. That's why I was imprisoned and sentenced to death. Thermidor, nine months later, spared me from the guillotine."

"Mon cher, my life is littered with errors despite my daily readings of our Kempis. I thought Russia was gestating the embryo of the new man, that free, fraternal, selfless being Christianity hadn't managed to forge after twenty centuries . . ."

"If you'd read what I'd published in 1794 and '95 against the Convention and Directoire you wouldn't have fallen into that terrible trap. Those who seized power in the name of the people couldn't take the sting of my criticism and used the Immigration Laws against me."

"What do you mean?"

"I mean, the one decreed later by the cloth-capped founders of Socialism to staunch the flood of Moors, Africans and South Americans . . . Worthy successors in fact to those who enslaved Indians and expelled Jews and Arabs!"

"Your anachronisms make my head spin. Let's return to when you went back to France. According to what I've read about you,

you became a herald for Bonaparte and a ferocious defender of the Empire."

"It was a sensible option, believe me. One had to choose between a constitution founded on natural right, that is, on the range of rights and duties of citizens in relation to the State, and the mayhem of a country at the mercy of a clerical rabble and a gang of inquisitors hiding behind invocations to the Virgin of the Pilar and the Fatherland: between being European or Kafirs. What's worse is that my fellow countrymen preferred to be Kafirs and still are however much they varnish themselves with the latest veneer."

"My dear abbot, one mustn't abandon hope. Things change and so do ideas. Reading our Founder's precepts has always enabled me to survive the most difficult times."

"I know the Cosa Santa to which you belong or say you belong performs like the Pope's pretorian guard and doesn't like reasoned debate or doctrines that can endanger the peace of the faithful; but doesn't that God they adore, that Inchoate Spirit encompassing eternity, ignoring the passage of time and filling the immensity of space, contradict their attempts to sign him up to an exclusive club? Dear Friar Bugeo (or should I call you by your inventor's name?), I prefer the Greeks' religion and immortal deities, swayed by human passions and extravagance. It's a less absolute, abstract belief, but infinitely more sensual and finally more enjoyable and diverting, don't you agree?"

"I concur with you on the literary plane. I translated the poet Cavafy a long time ago, and he was a devotee of the Greek gods, celebrating their amorous disarray in poems that delighted me until a band of clumsy imitators forced me to distance myself. However, I admire him and will continue to admire his courage."

"How do you marry a life— well— your carry-on, with a career in the church?"

(I don't know in fact whether I asked the question of Friar Bugeo or whether he anticipated it before I could put it into words.)

"*Homo sum: humani nihil a me alienum puto*. You know that better than I, though I'm sorry it made you give up the cloth. The Church has always shown extreme indulgence towards our carnal weaknesses. Just pass through the confessional and you're free of guilt. Trillions of Our Fathers and Hail Maries from penitents have redeemed countless souls of the pain of Purgatory!"

"Let the souls in Purgatory be! What you aver endorses the conclusion I reached after professing minor orders: the Church needs a cohort of docile functionaries, tormented by guilty consciences, all the better to maintain its power over them. Sin and confession, confession and sin are the Pontiff's most effective weapons in his project to enslave his flock's souls by dint of encyclicals."

"If consciousness of transgression and guilt vanished, what else would we have? Life would become awfully limp, my dear abbot."

"I'm not Friar Chastity Belt or the Devil Preacher, but I reckon clerical celibacy is an aberration. The greatest pleasure man has is in his dealing with the opposite sex, though I admit to exceptions as in your case as regards the targets of one's affections. From St. Ambrosio to St. Augustine, the fall-out from Rome's doctrine has been pernicious. Now that people are liberating themselves from that yoke, the Pope-Mobile tells us to recover our sense of sin; not a sense of civic responsibility in the body politic but abject submission to an entelechy contrary to natural law!"

Friar Bugeo looked at me. Or was it his author looking at me? The dubious authorship of this book confused me: after all that soul-swapping and historical upheaval the gloomy murk persisted: the mists weren't about to lift.

He suddenly told me about the May '68 events. He had paraded through Belleville after a theologian *molto aggiornato* and a group of transvestites dubbed the gasolines shouting *nous sommes tous des enculés*, and immigrants and bystanders applauded gleefully from the pavements. Then participated in the Odéon and Conservatoire National occupations: he came across Genet, Foucault, Severo Sarduy, Saint Juan of Barbès and numerous Sisters of Perpetual Succor. They floated on the air like bubbles until dismal reality pricked their dreams.

"I heard about the liberation of the Colegio de España and rushed to the University City. Three committees had already been created with political and administrative responsibility for the august building. I volunteered myself for the post of cultural facilitator and was unanimously elected. We debated in our assembly from dawn until dusk. Put the different proposals to an open vote and those adopted by a majority were inscribed in the statutes. Lived in a state of great excitement: *sous les pavés s'étendait la plage!* The Colegio would be a model for the libertian revolution! Perhaps you experienced equal euphoria after Robespierre's fall? Ours, *hélas*, was to be an ephemeral affair. In between assemblies and committees I organized a poetry soirée: there was a seer from the Spanish sticks, an inflictor of flinty verse who declaimed an ode to the Goals of the Sugar Harvest. The public applauded his catastrophic inspiration, but applause turned to whistles when a gasoline friend recited a languid, vaporous poem plucked from her sentimental bouquet. Insults rained down; someone lobbed a tomato smack in her face. I intervened but too late: the gasoline

sobbed and had to be carried to hospital. There was general agree-
ment on a vote as to how rooms in the Colegio should be distributed between revolutionary students: from sciences, arts, law and
medicine. Suddenly a beret-wearing refugee stood up; I'd spotted
him a few moments earlier, a Gauloise fag-end on his lower lip: If
I get your message, society in our country is exclusively made up
of young bourgeois who've been able to pay for their studies, or
am I mistaken? There were scattered protests but the fag-ender
pursued his harangue: The only genuine revolution is one politically led by the working class. We proletarians have the same right
as you to occupy recently liberated bedrooms. No one opposed his
thunderous argument: the rooms would be distributed between
students and workers, fifty-fifty. The fag-ender pursued his harangue:
I'm unsure whether à la Tallien or Marat. Perhaps, shitty *jeunesse
dorée*, you think the university elite comprises fifty percent of
Spain's population? Is this a representative democracy or a farce
manipulated by a handful of *nouveau riche* opportunists? The proletariat cannot compromise its egalitarian principles. As the immortal Bakunin said . . . His rhetoric inflamed tempers and insults
were traded. They accused each other of being Stalinists and yobs.
After a series of confabs and calls for consensus in honor of the
gloriously historical days we were experiencing, a committee was
set up to assign the rooms and beds available. The waters appeared
to have calmed but the sound of a single voice set them churning
again: and what about us? It was an austere, beautiful girl Roland
Barthes had introduced me to months earlier as a rigorous sup-
porter of *Tel Quel's* pro-China line. Men in rooms and women on
the street? A fine example of egalitarian democracy! Aren't you
ashamed to admit you're acting like macho pigs? Confusion spread:

squatters spoke or tried to speak at the same time, traded insults and accusations. A wag told an obscene joke about what women apparently wanted: to be flicked into the next planet. I tried to restore a little order and common sense, exhorted people to behave quietly and politely but all to no avail. The joker proceeded with his obscenities: he was drunk. Someone switched on the Hymn to the Republic at full blast."

(Friar Bugeo hummed along with the words of Espronceda's "Song of the Pirate.")

"Sorry if I'm interrupting you. But this music is so evocative, moves me deeply. When I finally managed to return to Spain after the uprising at Cabezas de San Juan the people of Madrid sang in the street not only the *Suck that then* but also these lines:

If priests and monks knew
what a beating we'll give 'em
they'd rush to the pulpit shouting
freedom, freedom, freedom!

These were heady days, never to be erased from my memory, though the clergy and most reactionary forces were waiting for an opportunity to wreak revenge and, helped by the Hundred Thousand Sons of that bastard Saint Louis and ecclesiastical mercenaries, after three years they re-established the tyranny of throne and altar. The possibility of a modern Spain, open to the winds of the change, evaporated. Fortunately, I perished before I saw it."

"What happened one hundred and forty-five years later came out of the blue. The majority of young girls and boys gathered in the Colegio in the University City were unaware of the hymn's symbolic value and began dancing, holding tight as if it were a *paso doble*. I don't know who'd had the brilliant idea of distributing beer and wine. The political debate dissolved into a rich broth of barracks humor, bull-ring bravado and bollocking. I don't know how it all ended since I walked out, intent on going home and sprucing myself up after two sleepless nights. However, luck or Providence decided differently. My petrol ran out (the service stations were closed) and I had to park my battered Volkswagen in the avenue de l'Opéra. I spotted a group of men and women I could immediately identify as Spanish from their dress and behavior. I thought they were heading to some trade-union or leftist demonstration (once, in my phase as a *mili-tante*, with my friends Succor and Support I'd joined an anti-racist demonstration and, when the bulk of the marching column added their own demands to the slogans agreed, my companions and I shouted festively: *augmentez LEURS salaires!*) But I discovered I was mistaken: they were heading to the branch of a Spanish bank on the opposite side of the road to withdraw their savings. There'd been an rumor they were going to devalue the French franc and it wouldn't buy a roasted chestnut! That was the final straw. I continued on foot to my house with Valle-Inclán on the tip of my tongue: Spain is a grotesque reflection of European civilization. As you wrote in one of your Bonapartist pamphlets, what can one expect of a nation which thinks poorly and writes vacuously?"

"I lived May '68 less on a high, more pragmatically: the years don't pass in vain! After a general meeting of our association, The New Girondins, I went to soothe my ardor with our common friend M.P., the lady who confessed to you after sinning with me."

"Yes, a delightful penitent—so witty. I think I mention her in my manuscript."

"Can I tell you an anecdote? One day she told me the joke she played on you before I introduced you and you became friends. You were on on one of your blessed cruises around Strasbourg-Saint Denis and she pretended to be on the job and asked you, *tu viens, chéri?*"

"Oh, and she tells you I replied *Si tout le monde était comme moi tu trimerais dans une usine, ma petite!*, but it's not true. I remembered the pious incident attributed to Monsignor and I told her: you're a brazen hussy, that's what you are!"

"Swings and roundabouts: in the end she chose you as a confidant while with me she intoned prayers and chants, from the *tantum ergo* to the *venite, adoremus*. For sure, I'd like to take advantage of this encounter which perhaps will only reoccur in hundreds of years to ask you to clear up a few obscure aspects from your revolutionary period . . ."

"I'd like to add, at the risk of seeming rude, that yours is hardly transparent. Enough comings and goings to bewilder Deep Purple's solid grey matter and provide ammunition for his researches and humorous sallies."

"What else do you expect from someone educated like myself in that French-loving, African Spain? Imitations of Europe's political and literary trends and fashions always fifty or a hundred years too late, always sailing behind the times . . . The experience acquired by those of us who emigrated to get some fresh ideas made no impact on jingoistic, Catholic navel-gazers. But it's grotesque to label our philosophical doctrines à la Diderot and Voltaire as retrograde when they're still defending the relevance of St. Thomas's syllogisms and *summas*, do you not think?"

"Let's put that aside for the moment. You know how in questions of faith I submit to the judgment of the Apostolic, Roman

Catholic Church with the utmost filial obedience. Monsignor, so forgiving of earthly pains and tribulations, does not permit the slightest doctrinal deviation."

"*Eh bien, changeons de sujet!* Is it true, my dear Father Trennes, that you were bagged in a roundup of fairies on your stay in Havana and were wickedly penned up in a cell full of headcases and Contra agents who nearly lynched you when you told them you didn't know why you were there as you were a Castro-ite and revolutionary? Someone told me . . ."

"The protagonist of that miserable episode was my friend Virgilio Piñera! I was a progressive priest à la Ernesto Cardenal (although I never perpetrated poetry outside my translations of Cavafy) and was, in a manner of speaking, beyond good and evil. I stayed in a suite at the Habana Libre and received the full honors of a Vatican dignitary. I still don't know who paid the bill for my infinite Daiquiris and Cuba Libres!"

We returned to Deep Purple and his aspersions on my life. Unable to suppress a smile, Friar Bugeo evoked the incident of my jailing in the Conciergerie, with Riouffe and other Girondin comrades. As I trawled memory's alleyways, he surprised me by declaring that his recollections were even starker.

He got up from his seat, took a copy of the second volume of the *History of Spanish Heterodoxy* from the shelf, and looked for the chapter attacking me until he came to page 639. He sipped water to clear his throat and read aloud:

> *A poor Benedictine lived in the dungeon where they were locked up, a poor, saintly, most patient man whom they delighted in tormenting a thousand exquisite ways. They stole his breviary, they blew out his light, they interrupted his devout prayers by chorusing some obscene ditty. The unhappy monk bore it*

all with resignation, offering those tribulations to God, and never losing the hope that he would convert those soulless folk.

He broke off. *Un ange passa* (or perhaps an archangel). He took another sip of water. "I am that Benedictine. I've lost count of my transmigrations, but I can assure you it's true."

"Should I then beg your forgiveness for our jokes and irreverencies?"

(Father Trennes—or was it the Benedictine monk?—seemed to be the victim of galloping senility. He was shedding his leaves like an old tree. His wrinkles, freckles, discolored patches of skin, wisps of grey hair, faded blue eyes, belonged to a man more than two centuries old. His brittle parchment hands could hardly bear the weight of my rabid detractor's tome.)

"My son, the experience I've accumulated ever since makes me see things differently. In truth, the jokes and pranks you played enabled me to suffer that test. Your ceremonies devoted to Ibrasha (or was it Abraxás?) were extremely amusing."

"What an excellent memory you have! We wrote a prayer to you though I forget the words. At that time I was very rude, a real priest-hater. My twisted biographer is right when he says you suffered our japes with Christian resignation."

"What else could I do in the middle of that hubbub? You acted like ten-year-olds! But the tohu-bohu made us all forget we were in the cell of those sentenced to death in the name of the Goddess Reason."

"Oh, the ups and downs of life, dear Friar Bugeo! Anyway, I'm pleased to know you bear me no grudges. The portrait Deep Purple Don Marcelino drew of me, with a blowtorch rather than a pen stopped people from reading my work and gleefully allowed them to repeat his diatribes without bothering to refer to his sources. And thus is history writ!"

"Don't complain about your fate. Things have gone much better for you in the century just coming to an end. Your ideas about tolerance and civic behavior have triumphed in many countries, even in Spain! Nobody is now shocked by what you wrote two hundred years ago."

"Not even your colleagues in the Cosa Santa?"

"Now see here. We've adapted to the times and cheerfully accepted political and economic liberalism. Our activity is restricted to the religious and spiritual sphere:"

I closed my eyes for a moment (the light from the lamp was troubling me) and, when I reopened them, I discovered a Friar Bugeo rejuvenated by his author's feints and sleights-of-hand. He had anticipated my intention to give an outing to the book on "The Holy Mafia," for he left me with bile on my lips.

"Monsignor reconciled Spanish Catholicism and high finance and thus made a decisive contribution to Spain's modernization. Even Saint Juan of Barbès admits as much in one of his essays! Technocratic colleagues occupied leadership posts in universities and banks while you conducted sterile debates in the cafés of the Quartier Latin. We were the motor of change. I well remember the meetings of the Ruedo Ibérico group you attended. Words, words, words! They struggled against censorship and the day it disappeared, you disappeared. History is oblivion, dear abbot. I realized as much and abandoned you to your eternal wranglings to forage the Gare du Nord for saintly inspiration."

"I trust you met up with the one of your canonized brethren."

"The Lord never foresakes me! I spent the whole night in prayer with one until dawn awoke us."

"Was he one of the fiery souls portrayed in your manuscript?"

Father Trennes sighed: clearly he was affected by the exhausting transmigrations his creator had forced on him.

"There were so many that I left the majority in the inkpot! Besides, Saint Juan of Barbès couldn't bear his disciple outstripping him on his own territory! He bawled loudly and I had to break off my narrative."

8 ADVICE AND A DRUBBING FOR FATHER TRENNES

1

Fear of Ms. Lewin-Strauss and her acid commentaries on his manuscript had led him to conceive the idea—as base as it was opportunist—of extending the transmigrations with a series of heroines, from Diana and other errant, ambiguous shepherdesses. He thought of Alférez the Nun, whose virago state allowed her to compete with males and to triumph using identical weapons, of Agustina de Aragón transformed into an artillery woman (what a symbol!) for her love of the fatherland (shouldn't it rather be the motherland?), and then silenced (as more recently in Ibero-America) by the swashbucklers on her own side. Of Mariana Pineda, immortalized by Lorca. Of Sister San Sulpicio, wonderfully played by Imperio Argentina in the film he saw in his childhood in the the Jesuit school of St. Ignatius: dancing without cap or wimple to the sound of castanets and the guitar . . .

(Then he reincarnated, Father Trennes wickedly confided in me, as the Guardian Angel of the Most Holy Trinity, of the Sacred Heart of Jesus and Holy Innocents, that pinnacle of Spanish letters who entered La Cartuja after an amorous fall-out on conscript duty with a canteen flirt and, in the peace and serenity of the cloisters, just like the actress, fizzed in a whirl of *bulerías* and *fandangos*. The refrain was tailor-made: Little Fairy, don't eat beans, for you're a little girl and you'll cop the lot!

"Now she's like the Virgen del Carmen who gets an outing and airing on the maritime procession in Puerto Banús, the one whose chapel is usually the most visited during the Royal Fair of Madrid."

I told him such efforts would be onerous and futile. Someone would always criticize him according to the ideological trends of the day. Forty years ago I was rebuked because of the proletariat's minuscule role in my fables and, particularly, their lack of positive heroes. It wasn't good enough to express your hatred of the exploitative bourgeoisie to which your family belonged: you must infuse belief and hope in the working class, bolster its political consciousness, open its eyes to the light approaching from the East, etc. Our mutual friend Gil de Biedma had to listen to the same tune until he sent them all packing in a famous article. Now, those voices have gone silent, but others equally vitriolic and strident cry out. Why don't you denounce *tout court* the backwardness and oppression of women in the retrograde societies you like so much? Writing those occasional articles of yours doesn't free you of the obligation to write clearly on such issues in your elitist novels! Follow the examples of Talima Nasrim and Fatima Mernissi! And if the professor from California goes quiet, the professor from Oxford steps forward. Your representation of homosexuality seems at best equivocal: it suffers from passivity and masochism, borders on complicity with ancestral dominant powers-that-be. Like your friend Genet, you poetically exalt criminal hoodlums and thuggish bodyguards. You are, or say you are, a confirmed democrat, but contradiction and ambivalence nourishes your literary work. Your characters lack the pride and consciousness of today's militants, don't communicate radical political options to the gay reader or incite him to defend his rights: marriage, legislation for couples, entry into the army . . . In a word, you shoot off in every direction, then cast alienation in an irremediably alienated form."

Father Trennes contemplated his manuscript, his heart manifestly in his mouth.

"What should I do then, according to the authorized opinion of the Moorologist, the Saint of Barbès?"

"Elemental, my dear Friar Bugeo! Always follow the devout inspiration of your Kempis. Monsignor's maxims are a gold-mine and their exploitation shouldn't be simply left to psychoanalysts from the Sorbonne and Lacan's merry band of disciples."

2

During his stay in New York—sent, he claimed by the Cosa Santa on an undercover, operational mission—he went in my stead, uninvited, to a soirée at Manuel Puig's with other fairies of motley feather and fortune.

(Some time ago I'd noticed his presence in the Village where he followed me everywhere absurdly disguised as an executive, postman and even as a boot-and-belt merchant from Christopher Street. He would stalk some twenty meters behind me, in a blond wig, false beard or mustache, smoked specs, and if I stopped to observe him, he'd freeze and stick his big nose into some shop-window display of African masks or a yoga or aerobics center. He'd trip on my heels en route to the bathhouse in Saint Mark's Place, the cinema on Fourteenth Street or the dens I was drawn to, and later I'd see him, the tormented soul in the penumbra of what he dubs his novenas and saintly exercises. On another occasion when I chanced into Harlem and penetrated, quite fearfully, a sauna as sultry as its customers, to the point that a whitish patch betrayed my presence in the promiscuous darkness, minutes later I spotted another wan, pallid shade and realized it was him. Sometimes, fed up with his obsessive harassment, I'd swing round and confront his obtuse, infantile visage. At such moments, he'd pretend not to understand Spanish and stammer: I'm sorry, I don't understand your language, in his wretched English, like a bewildered Martian just landed on our planet. You've not the slightest sense of direction! Despite your daily dose of Monsignor, you lose your way at every step. When you leave the cinema, your saint goes to your head, and you don't know whether Union Square is on the right or left. If you want to poke around other people's lives, you must be able to meld into the landscape, take on local color, acquire a chameleon's invisibility. And you, sir, are like a Sumo wrestler in a rococo parlor full of miniatures! Can't you get on with your own life and let me be? Father Trennes wiped the sweat from his brow, removed his false beard and smiled ingenuously. You're right, our Kempis advises us to act wisely and discreetly. Forgive me if my huge affection for your person seems overbearing. I'll head straight back to the Cosa's oratory and, like Sheherazade, recite the Thousand Less One Maxims by our blessed Founder!)

Manuel had phoned to invite me to his party but, when I saw Friar Bugeo parked on the corner watching for my every movement, I hid in the next-door lobby and, greatly relieved, let him head on up to the apartment for the happening.

M.P. informed me weeks later what happened in a missive written in French which I translated into an elegant Spanish, as respectfully as I would the letters of Madame de Staël.

3

The Argentine author you advised me to read was all over me when I congratulated him on the success of *The Buenos Aires Affair.* He told me he was organizing a surprise party that very afternoon for people of every sex and age. You can bring anyone you want, even your lap-dog or Flaubert's parrot. We'll be a dozen or so novices and midwives: it will be my very great pleasure to introduce you to the one and only Rita Hayworth.

It was verily a memorable soirée, and some other time I'll give you chapter and verse on our host's exquisite arts as an impersonator and his inimitable imitation ('scuse my gaucherie) of the dance from *Gilda* to the film's soundtrack. Néstor Almendros took photos and promised to send a few as mementos. I trust he won't forget me.

I counted a few of your friends among the party guests, Succor and Support, Sarduy's inseparable sisters, as well as Manuel's American translator and two professorial intimates of yours, called Linda and Gloria, if my memory doesn't deceive me. The latter sings in a piano bar and specializes in Puerto Rican literature.

Last but not least, I knocked into the inevitable Father Trennes, as flushed and gauche as ever, although he tried to hide his clumsiness under a carefree, festive veneer.

Him: As Cervantes would say, you're a lady for all seasons and seasoning, but don't try me with quince, figs or fruit, they don't appeal even in a painting! You know by now that my scene . . .

Me: We are kindred spirits, Father. Though my tastes are less plebeian than yours . . . Rugged, certainly; lively and persistent, as well; but distinguished chaps with a good share portfolio in the bank.

Him: I remember your troubled soul's daydreams: well-built, rich, tilting a hefty lance . . . Do you really think such miracles exist in that wretched world hurtling to inexorable destruction because of our enormous sins?

Me: At my age (just turned twenty) I'm happy if they only stick my nightingale in their cage. Just like you, Father.

Him: Oh, I'm but a worn-out relic! Only my faith keeps me erect.

(By the way, one of the party-goers recounted an anecdote—you can tell me if it's true—attributed to our Father. Evidently he was waiting in the late hours of the night for a saint to pitch up at a central stall in a boulevard Rochechouart chapel. It was winter, snowing and nobody turned up for prayers. But he lingered in his tabernacle, hoping against hope, while a young Cosa Santa colleague, tired of standing guard outside to ward off possible dangers, reprehended him respectfully: *voyons, mon père, soyez sage, il est tard, il fait froid, personne ne viendra avec un temps pareil!*

Is this a true story? I later heard another version, featuring a famous composer.)

After the *Gilda* dance and routines by Succor and Support, in plaits and little Shirley Temple numbers, we settled down in a corner. Father Trennes looked at me anxiously. He'd sent his draft manuscript days ago (make sure you don't show it to Saint Juan of Barbès!) and was sheepishly awaiting my verdict. Well, what can I say? The simple listing of your pick-ups and unholy places is a turn-off if it's not transformed via parody and humor. My catalogue of loves beats yours — (I counted more than five hundred on one sleepless night!) — but a prolix account would bore third parties, however wondrous the feats. Naturally, I could relate the ways I deflate my preening fighting-cocks; you're well-equipped, but you rush it; you've never met the body of a randy turkey-hen like me; you boast about length and forget about diameter; you're a real know-it-all but should go back to basics, etc., and so I declare my independence and superiority. My feminism is all about taking up arms and not being taken. Am I a non-praying mantis? Why not? I prefer nymphomania to the nimbomania of those aspiring after saintly haloes, Reverend Father. If you don't have the Kamikaze push like me, have recourse to a jester's tricks and wiles and put them in your autobiography. Turn the discourse of the Blessèd One and his brood inside out, like a sock!: we, discreet, unlettered sisters mentioned by your Kempis, and you, lasses setting out your stall with a sashay and a ditty, will come out tops. Tear up all you've done and in its place write a *Bitecomédie* or a Zobi *comedia* like the one Friar Bugeo wrote to the greater glory and mickey of Don Diego Fajardo's cock!

His day was as long as a day without juice from the syringe! I saw him age and collapse like freshly fished, obese hake. Perhaps I was too cruel and direct, but his credulity put me in a lather. The abbot you refer to a few pages back, whom I met in May '68, boasted he was a consummate Don Juan but wasn't worth a corn-

flake! However, I don't want to bore you with my New York rem-
iniscences. Manuel, Néstor and their friends send greetings to you
in your refuge in Tangier. By the by, haven't you come across
Severo in the Small Souk or the Cervantes Theatre? Succor and
Support told me he was making a hit there with François and the
Semiologist. The local flock must be red-hot stuff. What a fine
plethora of saints!

4

After the collapse of the utopias and discourses with which we
deluded ourselves, when Father Trennes lost interest in me and
abandoned me to my destiny, I took refuge with half a dozen ex-
gasolines in a little house in Nanterre.

Our project of total revolution had failed; feeling fragile and
abandoned, we decided to live in a commune, but jealousy and
rows soon put an end to that and we each went our way.

Suddenly I had no cash or work, I prostituted myself, began to
go downhill, only the illusion I was a woman brought me a blast
of oxygen, I wanted to collect the sum necessary to excise my
penis and twin baubles, and although the friends approached
turned their backs on me, after much heaving and blowing I managed the sum demanded by the super-specialist (the Argentinian
doctor suggested by M.P.).

I remember how jubilantly I greeted the suppression of my
attachments on leaving the operation theatre, I was a transsexual!,
had visiting cards printed with my feminized name preceded by a
gorgeous Mademoiselle, also wrote a letter in Spanish and English
to my family in the Isles, your Pablo Armando Jr is now a Paulina,

intends to marry and have children, I hope to send you soon my photo in a Pronuptia outfit. I soared on a high beyond words, prayed to God for a proper fiancé, went to church, recited prayers, took communion two or three times a day, aspired to the delights of sanctity, it was a happy, optimistic phase suddenly interrupted by the tittle-tattle of an envious colleague (her operation had failed and she looked a real scarecrow) who spread the story in the entrance to the church where I dreamt of a white wedding. The faithful of Notre-Dame de Lorette began to look at me askance, I heard them murmur, look at those hands, her shoulders and collarbone aren't feminine, a transvestite, the cheek of it!, and they proceeded to give me a wide berth, steered clear, swapped knowing smiles. The hope of a husband that sustained me was definitively fucked, the parishioners scorned me and I had to stash in a cupboard *my* Kempis from Father Trennes, Catholic Action gear and Corpus Christi mantilla, I was repudiated by that self-styled Christian scum and my initial grief gave way to anger, henceforth I would live without thinking about them, would extract the best from life's juices, sell myself to the highest bidder, post messages in the personal ads page of Libération, I made contact with single men, widowers and paterfamiliases, with voyeurs and Peeping Toms of every kind, the one-syllable monster still hadn't shown itself and I felt emboldened, rejuvenated by my ploys, I dressed provocatively, miniskirts, lacy bras, high heels, lurid wigs, tired of corresponding with inept, flawed individuals I cruised the area between Clichy and Pigalle, sometimes spotted thereabouts Trennes and Saint Juan de Barbès en route to Madeleine's knocking-shop, I pointed them out to passersby, my mocking jibes pursued them, hope you get it good and hard!, got your tube of vaseline?, and so on for years and years, protected from the plague by trusty condoms and a pimp's discreet support until the early hours of the day I was attacked by a group of skinheads in military uniform, with liters of beer and rubber truncheons, what a whore, a real Madame Butterfly, we'll do her over, bawled their leader, he'd grabbed me by the arm and I could smell his stale, beery breath, come here darlin', we're on the razzle, you are goin' to have a great time, after the doin' over we'll give you not even your ma'll recognize you, they dragged me to a car, ignored my cries, nobody rushed to defend me, the witnesses of the rape looked on from afar or hurried along, four of them, four, the driver and three mates, those in the back seat squeezed my tits between their pigs' trotters, are they silicone or were you on hormones?, fuck!, he ain't got a nob, he's had an operation on the Welfare and they clobber us with taxes!, they ripped my dress open in the city center, laughed at my squeals, sing your disgusting chinkie ditty, it'll be your swan song!, a real nightmare, where's my pimp and the police patrols that usually do this district, who pull me, ask for my papers, put me on file time and again at the station? they'd vanished!, I was in the hands of a nazi gang, jammed between prying hands, the boss and the driver, where were they taking me and what were they going to do to me? I could see the shaven necks of the ones in front, pappy, greasy, too many fry-ups and hamburgers, Chicago Bulls t-shirts, piggy snouts, they headed off the ring-road to darker, more desolate areas finally halted next to wasteland, get on the ground, you queer, now you'll find out what chinks of your type have got comin' to them (they'd refused to listen to my pleas: I'm a Hispanic Philippine, a Catholic girl!), and they took it in turns to stick their sick, repulsive pricks in my arse before they kicked me in the teeth, broke two, threatening me again with a learn your lesson, if we see you back in Pigalle we won't give you the chance to tell your tale!, I don't know how I managed to get up and walk to the ring-road exit, it was daybreak and, in the anemic light, I could make out in my pocket mirror the extent of the disaster, two shiners, bleeding lips, swollen cheeks, streaming eye-liner, my appearance inspired horror not sympathy, my shouts of help didn't stir the drivers from their selfishness, some accelerated, others slammed on their brakes and then drove off, her pimp gave her a hiding, must be a settling of accounts between drug addicts or perverts, while I tottered, smashed up, a real ecce femina, until I found the police car, got to hospital, was seen in emergency, they took a statement, I denounced my attackers, they proceeded to a series of analyses and blood tests, I got psychiatric help, returned home a shadow of myself, in none of my transmigrations had I suffered a humiliation like it, I needed to go to the dentist, have my face reshaped, cohabit for the moment with my one-eyed, lop-sided image, I spent days shut up in my attic with another ex-gasoline, apprehensive about what might yet be in store, the results of the hospital analyses, the official confirmation that I was HIV positive, and it all turned out as I feared, I read and re-read the medical sentence, tore it into little bits, the psychiatrist prescribed a list of tranquilizers, advised me to face up to reality, to confront my misfortune courageously, *soyez forte, ne vous découragez pas, ne laissez surtout pas le suivi psychologique,* month after month I went robot-like from my den to his consultancy, from the consultancy to my den, with no perspectives or possibilities, when one day by chance I heard a radio program about the Saint Bernard's Church occupation and actions on behalf of society's cast-offs condemned like me to the margins, to clan-

destine existence, I finally saw a light shine, a glimmer of hope, as
they were fighting racism, I told myself, they'll do something for
me, a mestiza transsexual excluded on two counts, I put on the
flounced dress I wore twenty years before to the Luxor and headed
to Barbès, the customers on the metro moved away from me, but
a new pride and vibrant feeling of self-esteem encouraged me, I
wanted to join that identity protest, struggle tooth and nail against
the oppression in our hypocritical society, I introduced myself at
the improvised entrance to the church and set out my stall, first
gently, then shouting, the machismo and homophobia of eurocrats
had made of me an object of horror to the self-righteous, my mere
existence was a provocation, transsexual, Asiatic, HIV-positive,
nobody could deserve more help and solidarity than me, I was
ready to fight for myself and everyone else, to confront the nor-
malizing institutions and their dogs of prey, I spoke lyrically, ani-
matedly, recited an ecumenical poem by Ernesto Cardenal,
convinced my eloquence had got them in my pocket, so that when
the spokesman for those occupying the church suddenly let rip we
have too many problems with immigrants with no papers to
devote our time to transvestites, I dropped, as Succor and Support
used to say, off the altar, couldn't believe my ears, how could a representative of an organization devoted to fighting social exclusion
and poverty dismiss me so cruelly, so insensitively?, I felt I was back
in the wasteland where I'd been raped, turned round unable to
hide my tears, and there was the star bishop, would-be defender of
progressive, humanitarian causes, tubby, bespectacled, with queen-
ish grotesque twitches, opening like a flower to the light from the
television spotlights, you must forgive me, as you can see I've a
packed diary and no time to listen to you, and he left me quickly

to steal light like a befuddled moth, I tried to shout who are you, Monseigneur de merde, to treat me like this?, have you by any chance lived seven lives like me?, experienced the anguish of betrayal and torture?, did you have the privilege of visiting Saint John of the Cross in his dungeon in Toledo?, I wanted to slap a custard pie on his mug in front of thousands of viewers, that way he'd learn not to mock me and, like his peers, turn away from my sad state of abandon!, sons of a bitch, that's what they were!, I was choked, furious, how could I get my revenge?, on their indifference to my misfortunes, their cheap generosity, media pirouettes?, I hated them, really hated them!, I decided to puncture the tires of the cars parked nearby but, where to get a hammer and nails?, I did snap several car aerials, that'll teach you, you fucking pansy!, don't talk to me about humanitarian organizations!, I took refuge in the attic I shared with the other gasoline, completely hysterical and disheveled, I wanted to splatter them all like cockroaches, they'd find out who I was!, I started a campaign of telephone harassment against those occupying the church with cards my mate had snatched from a kiosk, I called them a hundred, five hundred times, hi! you the profiteers from pain?, the do-good jokers?, leeching on misery?, I changed my tone of voice so as not to be identified and met their disarray with guffaws and insults, get it in the arse like me, you wankers!, then used Minitel, ordered on their account all manner of articles from mail-order firms selling Armani suits, Iranian caviar, orchids, champagne, foie-gras, lingerie, luxury perfumes, pornographic films with S&M action, big-format dildoes, fifteen Child Jesuses from a religious shop in Saint-Sulpice, washing-machines, refrigerators, vibrators, whips, when the police tracked me down the charity-givers were in debt by over three hundred thousand francs, I ended up in the women's jail where I'm waiting to be sentenced in the special wing for those with the virus, loathing you to death, you hypocrite and pharisee, your sanctimonious selfishness, you're happy putting me inside or letting me die in a plague hospital, I'm sick of your bleating words of sympathy and wretched excuses, spread yourself over the pages of this book, go fuck your saints!

5

Ever since the divinely inspired creation of the Cosa Santa on October 2, 1928, the festival of the Holy Guardian Angels, we've been the object of all manner of attacks and slander, both in relation to our apostolic labors and to the person of our Founder. Penpushing mercenaries, wolves in sheep's clothing, deserters to enemy ranks have tried unsuccessfully, like people gobbing at heaven, to besmirch one and the other. We are used to these reactions of hatred and anger, sustained by our faith in Christ and the protection of his Vicar upon Earth, and we refuse to lower ourselves to reply to those undeserving even of our contempt. Give our silence as response and continue along the road, as our Father advises in our doctrinal breviary. But the infamous libel signed by "Friar Bugeo" beats all records for base abomination. Taking quotations and sayings imbued with modesty and evangelical spirit out of context, he manipulates them on behalf of a discourse which would be derisory if it weren't simply abject. Father Trennes who says he speaks in our names is totally unknown in the ranks of the Cosa which has today spread, thanks to the grace of our Lord, to the five corners of the world. The pseudonym behind which he hides and conceals his identity reveals no doubt his perfidious intentions and desire to muddy the Apostolic, Roman Catholic Church. The Monsignor's life was a model of courage, humility and modesty, as the process of his beatification has so well documented. We priests and lay members of the Cosa strive to follow his example by not letting ourselves be derailed by any campaign of lies and slander led by people who deny the Providence of God and offer themselves to the highest payer like common prostitutes. In these permissive times any felon can perpetrate his misdemeanors with absolute impunity: the law of the land doesn't punish those who pervert souls and live on the fruits of their amorality. But the author of that fetid freak will have an opportunity to meditate thereupon when he enters the timeless zone. Then will truth triumph: the wheat will be separated from the chaff. The light of the Holy Spirit guides us always and, as the Father says, with that philosophical profundity never plumbed by chip-on-the-shoulder merchants of Friar Bugeo's ilk, after seeing how many spend their entire lives (tongues, tongues, tongues, with all the consequences) silence seems ever more necessary and agreeable.

Ramón Garcia Montero, Professor of Administrative Law, calle Vesubio 74, Madrid.★

★ Letter sent to the publisher of this work after reading the proofs.

9 IN THE FAIRY CAFÉ DES OISEAUX

I met him or, rather, he found me in one of the Holy Places which
we frequented, where he'd follow me daily from chapel to chapel,
station to station, step by step, like a spy or private eye. His polic-
ing of my apostolic labors reached extremes that would be laugh-
able if they weren't so gauche and insufferable. Sometimes, if I
withdrew to meditate in one of the tabernacles of *gai-savoir* that in
days of yore lit up Paris's asphalt grey, I'd find him the other side of
the *Vespasienne* with his card-carrying Cosa Santa pippin-face, contemplating enraptured the elevated object of my devotions. My
dear Father Trennes, can't you do your own pick-ups and keep off
my shooting range? Can't you see, sir, that you get in my way and
derive no benefit from your impertinence? Your winsome, sanctimonious ways won't fish a miserable sardine! You are the worst sort
of voyeur: instead of Friar Bugeo you deserve to be called
Reverend Peeping Tom! Carry your own cross and don't turn into
one of mine!

But nothing would deter him from poking into my affairs,
whether in the boulevard Rochechouart, the Luxor cinema or station lavatories. We seemed like two inseparable but warring twins:
he aged with me, his facial features sagged, his hair started to thin.
This parody and caricature of myself bordered on obsessive delir-

ium: one night when I bumped into a saint of my private devotion he buzzed around us like a horsefly to the hotel on the rue Ramey, endlessly repeating the same old tune, his stupid refrain: What are we doing? where are we going? And I rapped him with my scissors: go and read your Monsignor à la Kempis and I'll see to my own business!

But that afternoon, Father Trennes was beside himself, like a child with a big secret or bringing a big piece of news.

"I've been looking for you on the boulevards, in the cinema or the teahouses of Barbès. Something unexpected has happened that will interest you as it concerns you and that book of yours. How about if we both had a chat on the terrace of the Fairy Café?"

I had no alternative but to accept and we walked silently to the Square d'Anvers. I made sure Genet wasn't there with Al Ketrani or some Palestinian militant. I ordered tea and my double ordered a Vittel. *Sans glaçons*, he emphasized. He waited for the waiter to serve us and take his tray away.

"My dear friend, I've been privy to a surprise encounter between two characters you know very well and have written screeds on. I could play at guessing-games but I won't wilfully prolong the suspense. It's about Deep Purple and . . ."

"I can see you fancy this saintly male. Didn't you run him dry when you confronted him with the libertine abbot?"

"Forgive me, he's one of Monsignor's favorite writers. He once confided to me that he was a precious guide against worldly temptations, the flesh and the devil. But this time he didn't converse with the abbot but with someone much closer to you: none other than Blanco White."

"Can you tell me, if it's not a secret like all the rules and deal-

ings of the Cosa Santa, where you ran into them? Was it the top
floor of the Royal Academy of History or Mr. Rathbone's estate,
whither Don José María Blanco retired before dying?"

"Neither. There I was meditating on our Founder's profound
precepts when they burst into my flat, taking advantage of the fact
I'd forgotten to shut the door after I'd signed for a registered letter.
I recognized them immediately: their dress and looks exactly
matched the photographs and engravings you showed me."

"How did the great defender of the faith treat you? Though he
was a fanatical Catholic, his devotion to the Jesuits led him to
regard the Cosa's innovations rather suspiciously, and privately he
would compare their organization and methods to the Spanish
neo-Hegelians he execrated."

"That was only at the beginning, when our competition with the
Company of Jesus was fiercer! In effect, I had heard that he'd stigma-
tized us as a lodge, a mutual benefit society, a fraternity, a monolith.
Deep Purple didn't hold back, but later he set things right. He
understood how the Cosa was a response to the needs of our time.
He even enthusiastically supported the cause of Monsignor's canonization, I don't know if you've cottoned onto that."

The dialogue of two such dissimilar, opposed characters had
aroused him to such a pitch that he recorded their words on a tape-
recorder without their noticing. They faced each other from the
armchairs of the three-piece that's already been described. Deep
Purple savored his excellent vintage Rioja whilst José María
Blanco sipped the Lipton tea brewing in the teapot. The Sevillian
looked his bitter, though admiring, detractor up and down. "I've
read all you've written about me: first a Catholic, then an
Encyclopedist, later a defender of the Anglican church and finally

a Unitarian, barely a Christian . . . Well, what's the point of continuing? A sectarian, ultra-orthodox interpretation, the real virulence of which, nevertheless, sparked in a few free spirits interest in my work, inducing one of them to translate it into Spanish, and you would no doubt have devoted a juicy chapter in your book to him if a lucky or unlucky star hadn't brought him into the world twenty years after you'd departed this earth. In a word, your rage at me bore late but real fruit. I owe it to you and I'd be a sad ingrate not to recognize that."

"You have to agree you've got more twists and turns than the labyrinth of Crete. A review of your life would sicken any reader in his right mind. I accept you're not one of those couch philosophers that make up so-called modern Spanish culture. For that very reason, your case is all the more serious. Pride and lust led you astray and shattered your soul's peace and quiet, though you only confess half as much in your Letters."

(Father Trennes' servile imitation of my voice and gestures irritated me. He spoke like me, expressed himself like me, wanted fusion with me. When I gazed at him, it was like gazing at a cruel caricature of myself.)

"Was this all a dream or a mere product of your imagination?"

"What does it matter either way? The essential fact is that they were there and I could see them just as I'm telling it to you. The two of them perching on the three-piece, as true-to-life as you and me! And I'd not been on hash or mescaline, like your much admired Artaud. I've been a man of sober habits ever since the Lord via his Divine Mediatrix, got me off alcohol for good after a series of derisory incidents that are irrelevant here."

I told him I liked disgressions and he caught my drift in a jiffy.

It was years after the episode narrated by Jaime of the soirée in his parents' luxury apartment on the calle Aragón which ended lamentably in back-street dives. I'd been invited to the USSR (in the days when I was a fellow-traveler or traveleress), to the commemoration of a titanic Caucasian poet by the name of Rustaveli. From morning to night the orators took the large theatre stage praising his magnificent, vigorous presence. It was simply unbearable: no need to have recourse to the headphones for the simultaneous translation, I could hear the litany of Dante, Shakespeare, Rustaveli; one orator (Alberta?) generously added the name of Cervantes to the triumvirate. The banquet organized by the local branch of the Writers' Union was but a series of toasts: the autochthons usually pour their wine or vodka into glasses made of auroch horn which you couldn't let go of or put down anywhere unless they were empty and, when that happened, one of mine hosts rushed to refill them. To peace, to friendship between peoples, to the Vietnamese resistance, to Republican Spain: the flow of wine was endless and I tried to slip away from the agape as soon as I could. But my pimpernel elusiveness was no help back in Moscow, on the eve of my return to France. I was staying in the Hotel Ukraine, next to a delegation of affable, smiling, teetotaling Vietnamese writers. Their spokesman had expressed his profound admiration for Spain and her people's heroic struggle against fascism. He had even published a poem on the subject and we agreed he'd give me a copy early the following day before flying to Hanoi. But Satan (sorry, I know you're not a believer!) wished it otherwise. I'd been invited to a famous Soviet writer's house (winner of the Stalin Fiction Prize, no less), a big drinker like most of his colleagues. We were served—them and me—in those appalling Georgian horns. As we toasted everything human and superhuman (Gagarin, the Sputnik!), I noticed my consciousness blurring, that I was entering a spongy alcoholic zone and my ears were being sealed with thick wax. I retain a confused memory of everything that ensued: random, as if chloroformed images, of my host's farewells; an unreal car-journey with my selfless minder; I hazily crossed the hotel lobby; threats and fisticuffs in the lift (as I later discovered, I tried to urinate there); finally my bedroom. I was still there a few hours later flat out on my bed, perhaps in the same position I'd collapsed into, when persistent loud knocking at my door cruelly roused me from my torpor. The ceiling heaved up and down, the furniture seemed to float on air, I rowed an inflatable dinghy, lashed by the waves. But the knocks still rained down and I finally left my skiff, forced my way through the tidal blast and fumbled with the key, fired by a desperate desire to obliterate the bloody early-riser: it was the Vietnamese delegation! For a few interminable seconds I examined the solemn, austere representatives of that people bombed daily by a deluge of phosphorous and napalm. I made every effort to assume a dignified stance in their eyes. The poet handed me a dedicated copy of his hymn to Spain. Was he going to launch into a speech?

The very thought caused me to shudder and I begged God to spare me that cup. The Vietnamese seemed to be waiting for my words of farewell but I felt unable to articulate a syllable. Perhaps they hadn't noticed my sad state and attributed my silence to pure emotion. Perhaps they read a vehement message of sympathy and solidarity in my bleary, blood-shot eyes. In any case I trust those minutes of agony on that dingy hotel corridor redeemed me from tens, nay hundreds of years we shall spend in the blessed Purgatory according to the Holy Church's doctrine. When they finally said goodbye to me, smiling and bowing their heads, mine was at the explosion point!

I'd read all this somewhere else and interrupted him: "I thought the Apostolic Prelature commissioned you to carry the image of the Virgin of Fatima to Russia in order to provoke the fall of Communism."

"Communism didn't need me or Our Lady to collapse by itself! Its ruin was already evident to species of curious bystanders like me."

"Why didn't your nosey-pokery extend the space occupied by the saintliness delineated in your manuscript?"

"By now you know as well as I do that my saints wear another cloth! Besides, the righteous society reigning there repressed our apostolic labors. A typically bourgeois aberration! They explained to me how it had all been swept away by the work of the Revolution. Nevertheless, I saw two or three of Succor and Support's rivals at the Bolshoi. They'd gone to see *Swan Lake* with Mayakovski's corpulent, very décolletée widow!"

"Let's return to the thread of your imaginary tale. We left it mid-diatribe by Don Deep Purple against my alter ego's life and work."

" 'Scuse me, I thought I was your alter ego!"

"You're only a parasite who lives off me without a smidgeon of thanks. Worse still: you're a patented, copyrighted plagiarist insinu-ating that I'm the one stealing your themes and subjects. If it weren't for the compassion your torpid incapacity arouses in me, I'd have sent you packing long ago back to Monsignor!"

"All right, don't get angry, I'll resume my tale. There were my characters, in their respective armchairs, *en se regardant en chiens de faïence* but, as soon as they appeared in my flat, almost imperceptibly, their faces became disfigured: they looked like children's magazine silhouettes that a reader or readeress must finish off in pencil. Fortunately, their accents were clear as a bell: Castilian, on the one hand, and Andalusian soaked in Thames water, on the part of the author you prologued and translated . . ."

Blanco: Don't you think the way you explain what you call my apostasy is rather summary? Neither sensuality nor pride head the list of my defects.

Purple: That's what you say now. But, if I stick to your own writing, I can prove how, though a priest, you lived immersed in immorality and were, to quote your own words, "burrowing into feminine virtue."

Blanco: At least I was honest enough to admit as much. Let him who walks guilt-free throw the first stone!

Purple: Perhaps you're not one of the crew of womanizing, concubinizing priests, led by their natural inclination to loose, wheeler-dealer lives, to hang up the cloth and become Mormons or Quakers. But a bit of skirt lurks behind every heresy!

Blanco: Don't let passion blind you. My life was the result of moral, intellectual anguish, the fruit of continuous self-dissatisfaction. What's wrong with that? The majority of our compatriots believed and killed one another in the name of their beliefs because they were incapable of thought. I'm not sure much has changed over the last thirty years.

Purple: Reason is important, but it has its limits. His Holiness just confirmed as much masterfully in his last Encyclical.

Blanco: Let's return to the issue of lechery, which is at the center of your attacks. If my memory doesn't deceive me, you accuse me of fathering several children; and because I loved the fruits of my sins, you say, I tried to give them a name and social status: hence my decision to emigrate and turn Protestant.

Purple: You think one religion's as good as any other and changed yours as it suited you. As for your children . . .

Blanco: My son, born in my Madrid period that I describe in *The Letters*, I arranged for my nearest and dearest to send him to England where he enlisted years later in the East India Company. The others—the plural is yours, sir—are purely and simply your invention . . .

Purple: I'm sorry if that's the case. In an enterprise as vast as mine one has recourse to the sources at one's disposal and if these are inaccurate, the odd error slips in unnoticed. But my slip of the pen doesn't absolve you from your most grave sinning and wrongdoing against the faith and righteous behavior.

Blanco: I can see you maintain the holy fervor which won you tumultuous, rather than honorable, renown in the National-Catholic Church and among the zealous. I don't dare think what apologies and proclamations you might have written in Franco's barracks in Burgos had you lived the three years of the Crusade. The wretched propensity with which our countrymen spill their blood, for want of anything else to spill, revisited and outdid the horrors I witnessed during the Napoleonic invasion. Except for two worthy exceptions, your cardinals and bishops blessed the massacre and proclaimed the slaughterer-in-chief, Caudillo of Spain, by the grace of God. You were lucky to be born in 1856 and to avoid getting caught up in the dirt from the victors' repressive machinery. In all likelihood they'd have appointed you Director General of the Press and Propaganda!

Purple: Revolutionaries, dear Mister White, always cultivate the nether regions of human nature. Any ideal of liberty, equality or progress triumphs and takes root in the masses if it's entwined with self-interest and envy, the determining factors in the philosophy of history.

Blanco: By enforcing the inhuman dogma of clerical celibacy, the Church of Rome condemns itself to see the world through the prism of sex. But what you throw out the door, jumps in via the rear window. You have Midas's awesome power: everything you touch turns to lechery and sin. Haven't you read *Millenari*'s press revelations on the Vatican's secret sewers and carry-ons?

Purple: Slander, libels as old as the world, my dear Blanco! The Church's sacred body is above such malicious gossip!

Blanco: In my *Algerian Dialogues* I proved how divine law cannot oppose natural law, let alone abrogate it . . . Better marry, than burn!

(Father Trennes sighed: "My dear girlfriend M.P. said to me the other day on this subject: 'Oh, you know, these days, only priests are interested in marriage,' and I think she got it right about the fancies of a goodly number of them . . ."

My double laughed as if scared by his own audacity: "Well, my dear Juan, though I scrutinized this little opus against clerical celibacy, I didn't find a single reference to the holiness you and I preach."

What was the point of his morbid desire to have me as eternal witness to his coarse, half-cock imitations?)

"For Christ's sake, get to the end of your dream or half-baked invention! You'd left Deep Purple and your heresiarch face-to-face on the armchairs of your three-piece . . ."

"Forgive me. I gave them a break so one could pour out more wine (best vintage Rioja!) and the other could sip more tea. The

two sat as stiff as a couple of wax figures from Madame Tussaud's."
Purple: Has that Irish stew they call modern or postmodern Spanish culture given you a space among the strident chorus of radio station and Channel Four pundits?
Blanco: My media presence is more than a tad modest. Recently, a real-life Professor published a book on nineteenth-century liberal thought and I don't even get a look in. But Spain is the fatherland of stuff and nonsense.
Purple: Don't confuse things, blinded by rancor. Rebel, restless spirits like yours will all emigrate to Europe and North America, just as in the happy days of the dictatorships.
Blanco: Perhaps you're right. Anyone who lives and thinks there according to his own lights and doesn't abide by the required norms is still a strong candidate for exile.
Purple: No political hooligans, democratic government or news media can eliminate our people's profoundly Catholic spirit. The devil made flesh, dressed as a woman, will only sink her teeth into feeble souls like yours.
Blanco: The sixth yet again, the *cherchez la femme* and damning of those dear disturbers of the clergy's peace!

(Father Trennes broke in: "I don't think your favorite author was really aware of the lives and works of our saints, do you?"

Without bothering to answer, I urged him to wind up the story before Genet showed his face in the café—I imagined the contempt the Father would arouse in him and his acid commentaries on his profession—or that Succor and Support would suddenly show with luscious blue-tinted, electrified locks.)

"Well, all right, my composition concludes very beautifully. The two were exhausted after so much chin-wagging (three-quarters remains in the inkpot!) and they finally launched into verse that will sound familiar to your ears."

Blanco: Tell me, sage vicar,
who set the principle
that eating an apple
made man a sinner?
Purple: The fault's the forbidden
fruit that's sweeter
what's tasty is sin
virtue is ever bitter
Blanco: Vicar, with your doctrine,
you must be a great sinner:
or so proclaims the odor
wafting from your kitchen.

Severo came over in a flash to say hello, en route to a date in Madeleine's hotel celebrated by Jouhandeau. Yesterday I read your chapter on "The Aftermath of a Shout" and, as I skimmed it, I felt I was reading myself. It is *un morceau de bravoure*, a beautiful homage. But let's return to that some other day: now I'm in a real rush! Soon after, Saint Juan of Barbès, no doubt jealous of my narrative designs, rudely interrupted this tale: he had spotted Abdullah on the boulevard, and eager for an opportunity to worship, was heading at top speed to the public tabernacle where, with saintly shamelessness, he wanted to exhibit his mace.

10 THE LAST SHOWDOWN

Father Trennes' obsessive self-identification with me deepened by the day. He waited for me by my front door, pursued me on my strolls through the neighborhood, followed me into the stores where I went shopping and mimetically chose the same garments, cleaning agents, tubes of toothpaste, bottles of mineral water. He painstakingly pushed his trolley behind mine and checked that the price of our purchases was identical. I found him in the chemist's, in the metro, at the pick-up points I preferred. When I thought I'd given him the slip and began to breathe easily, I suddenly perceived his presence in the penumbra of the Luxor, in the passageways of the hammam on the rue Voltaire, in the vicinity of the urinals on Stalingrad, Barbès and the boulevard Rochechouart. He also tried to pitch up, despite his dismal, disheveled appearance, with the woodsmen who interested me, he pretended to bump into us, escorted us to the rue Ramey hotel, to Madeleine's rented rooms. He tried to distract me from the task of bedding one of his "saints" with a fabulous yarn of his encounters with authors and characters about whom I've written or tasteless gossip about famous writers. Just imagine how yesterday I was in London with the journalist Juan Cruz and on the pavement in Gloucester Road, we came across an envelope addressed—have a guess!—to no less a person than one Mister Blanco White and the correspondent of the newspaper you work for kept it so he could deliver it by hand when he sees you, isn't that really extraordinary? Or: I went to see Deep Purple in his flat on the calle León and asked what tasty song and dance the womanizing abbot had got up to but which he'd left out of his reference work in order not to lower the tone. Or: I turned up at Cernuda's flat in Santa Mónica, with a letter of introduction from Gil de Biedma, and saw the photo of the youthful subject of the *Poems for a Body* (a very beautiful Mexican Italian). You must know our great poet hadn't heard of Cavafy? I brought him up to date and read him his poetry in my translation, the one I handed to Jaime before it was published in *Boteghe Oscura*. Or: did you know Truman Capote seduced Camus? At least that's what he said, though Gore Vidal told me the would-be affair was pure wishful thinking. But Mauriac was certainly one of the in-crowd: Roger Peyrefitte told me one day when he visited the Apostolic Prelature . . . At other times, even more fancifully, he declared he'd bedded Lorca and accompanied André Gide to a male brothel in Biskra. I had to gather all my steam to silence his intrusive lip and get down to my own business in the hourly rented rooms of the 18th *arrondissement*!

She flounced with the pink-soutaned seminarist or the over-the-top Philippiner in the gods at the Luxor, stirring it with fans and titters and stopping my own show in her stride. She strutted the rooms and passages of the baths in a nurse's white uniform, to all the world a be-toga'd senator, planted herself behind the door to the cubicle where I was finishing off my Turk and took a peep through the keyhole. She'd phone at midnight, not bothering to apologize, to relate some anecdote or other. I had to change numbers several times and leave the phone off the hook before I switched off the light.

When I tried to put land and sea between us, I'd secretly book my ticket, pick it up at the airport and, after checking he wasn't on the horizon, I'd breathe a sigh of relief. But my luck didn't last long, once on board the plane, I'd see him in the line of passengers waiting their turn to find a seat and put their bags and cases in the luggage compartment. My very own ghost-writer settled down by my side without a single blush: contiguous seats quite by chance. What a delightful surprise, my dear friend! So you're also off to Tangier! It's some time since I saw old friends like Roditi, Brion Gysin and George Lapassade. Do you know whether Genet still stays at the Minzeh or if he's set up in Larache? I've heard great things about an autobiography by one Choukri, that Paul Bowles has translated into English. Have you read it? As soon as we arrive I'll track down a copy in the Librairie des Colonnes. You're a friend of the Gerofi sisters, I suppose. Who doesn't know the Gerofi sisters in Tangier! What!, you've never heard of them? *Pas possible!* Doesn't a honorary Tangerine like you go to their bookshop? Allow me to say I don't believe you. They're the engine driving Tangier's intellectual life! I've never heard such a whopper! And so on, from take-off to touch-down for more than two hours.

What had I done to deserve this? That's what I asked myself as the taxi drove me to the city along the Cape Spratell highway. My cross—he really was the cross in my life!—had lost sight of me and I urged my driver to speed up, jump the lights, with the bait of a generous tip. I began to breathe once more, unpack my luggage, divide up my clothes and books between wardrobes, shelves and cupboard and acclimatized myself as if I were going to take root there.

(In my bag, I'd brought a copy of the Kempis in order to satirize Friar Bugeo's devotions and hoist him with his own petard.)

The delicious truce was short-lived. Father Trennes encountered me by chance in the Café de Paris or in the cafés on the Small Souk and terraces opposite the station. If he saw me reading a book or leafing through the foreign press (his country's was timeless, the headlines and photos never changed, the years stood still) he'd sit down some way away, but when he noticed the good company I was in, he'd sidle over carrying a volume of Cavafy's complete works or Mohammed Choukri's book.

"I didn't want to bother you, but I'd appreciate your opinion on a passage in Bowles' English version. May I sit down for a minute with you?"

"Reverend Father, for once and for all get off my back! This gentleman and I are not here to discuss translations. There's a time for everything and yours is to clear off right now."

"Well, do forgive me. I find your ideas and insights so precious. But I can wait until tomorrow. You'll be going for a coffee at the usual time?"

"Routine is no rozzer. Do whatever your sphincter tells you!"

That very afternoon I spotted him from the window, waiting for me to make my appearance with Buselham, Lakdar or the Tetuani regular at the Café Fuentes. No way could I throw him off: I met his mug, at night, around the Hotel Astoria bar, on the pavement outside the Carroussel, in the entrance to Le Monocle or the exit to Marco Polo's.

"Aren't you afraid you'll catch cold at the time of night? The Tangier climate is very treacherous!"

"I'm well wrapped up!"

"Rather than pointlessly tramping after me, you'd be better off going to a chemist's and buying aspirin."

"Don't you worry about my health! I'm watching over yours!"

He pursued me on every trip. Stumbled on my heels in Khan Al Khalili and the Fatimid district, set up stall on the cat-filled terrace of the Rich restaurant, spied on my dealings with a mustachioed falucca boatman and immediately reached his own with another (usually, ugly and ungainly), in the wake of our ride through the river's majestic, nocturnal silence. In Istanbul, I bumped into him in the Great Bazaar, in the steep streets of Beyöglü, in the area around the Pera Palas, whilst I walked arm in arm with my warlike wrestler from Smyrna. His total ignorance of the languages I command (his, he said, were Classical Greek and Aramaic) cut him out of the game and, visibly frustrated, he'd stop asking my companion questions and butt into our conversation about the Antalia or Bursa joints.

"Will you dine in the Haci Baba?" (Pathetically he pronounced AZI as HASHEY.)

"That's none of your business! If you're not inspired by reading your Kempis, then buy yourself a copy of Gala's *Turkish Passion!* You won't be able to put it down!"

"I was only asking because the most famous writers in the city usually dine there."

"When I've got a bodyguard, I couldn't give a sunflower seed for the literati, Reverend Father."

There was no escaping him: ridicule bounced off his tenacious hide. The more I strove to cut him out of my life and writing, the more he clung on. When I looked at myself in the mirror, I could see him transformed into a poor imitation or simulacrum of myself. Once when in sweet conjunction with one of the characters sketched in his manuscript, I became aware of his silent presence in a corner of the rue Ramey hotel. He was inspecting me, or inspecting himself, green with envy, as covetous as Melibea's serving-wench when she coupled with Calisto. Who had given him the key to the room? How could he have slipped in if we'd slammed the bolt too? He wasn't even masturbating like a vulgar Peeping Tom, but his lips were slavering. His hands and mouth were shaking. Was he praying for me? Cursing me? Reciting the Our Father or Monsignor's maxims? Impossible to say: he stayed put, spied on my rider's movements and attentions, impressively tactile. I don't know whether my warrior saw him, since he made no comment. When we'd finished the task in hand and he went to wash in the lavatory, Father Trennes had vanished. The door was still locked and bolted. I went home perplexed, not knowing whether my shadow's odious intervention was simply a hallucination or, as I'm inclined to think, a hard-edged reality.

Back in Barcelona, after a series of visits to Gil de Biedma's family apartment, to the basement on Muntaner and even the plush office at the Tobacco Company's, I decided to gather together all my friends — though most had died. I wanted them to witness my confrontation with Father Trennes, my face-out with my indefatigable pursuer, to clarify once and for all who'd copied who, who'd free-loaded, who'd plagiarized.

First I invited the poet and Gabriel Ferrater, Cuckoo and Pigtail, my publisher and his friend and then extended the summons to my New York and Parisian witnesses: Severo Sarduy and Néstor Almendros, Succor and Support, Manuel Puig and the Semiologist. M.P. sent his apologies: he was going on a Caribbean cruise with some kind of John Kennedy millionaire, a freckled red-head. I didn't even attempt to broach the matter with Genet for I could anticipate his response: *vous me faites chier avec vos histoires de tantes!*

The most difficult bit was getting hold of Friar Bugeo himself. He'd moved house, changed his telephone number, not let on his new details to anyone. After many fruitless queries, someone told me he was "imparting" a few classes on marketing techniques in the Marbella Enterprise Park. What the hell was he doing there?

"Our social labor must begin with businessmen, bankers and company directors. They are the engines pulling the carriages in this blessed heyday of neo-liberalism. The Apostolic Prelature has entrusted me with a proselytizing, pedagogical mission: the commerce of souls!"

Was he pulling my leg?

"I'm being perfectly serious. There are more than a hundred executives enrolled on my course. They are our future ministers. I can assure you I'm not coping."

"Please come, if only for a few hours. I need to clarify certain things with you with a group of common friends."

"Don't be impatient! I must preside over the Masters' graduation ceremony."

"When?"

"In a few weeks' time. Give me your fax number."

He was visibly afraid of such an encounter. This man, my double, or the shadow I couldn't shake off, piled up the obstacles, alleged vital commitments and a congested diary, paraded as a super-busy prof., overwhelmed by the burden of his titanic responsibility. It's otiose to add that his pretexts and evasions irritated me.

"How many women have enrolled on your courses, Reverend Father?"

"None. Monsignor prescribes the strict separation of the sexes. As he used to tell us before ascending to heaven, they don't need to be clever. Only discreet."

"Don't you think it all smells rather rancid?"

"Let them empty pillowcases! Knowledge would only be their ruin."

Sometimes he recorded his transcendental messages on the answering machine.

"The spiritual indoctrination of laymen must be the first step, in accord with the designs of Providence, in the Church's reconquest of its former worldly power."

"Social classes, each in their corresponding place, configure the order established by God in the Universe."

"If Christ were preaching today, he'd be dressed like an executive from the Marbella Enterprise Park."

Were his new technocratic convictions sincere? Had "Castro's Abbess," nicknamed thus by Almendros, thrust his missal and Kempis into the fiercest bastions of the school of the Chicago boys? Although I was past shock and pain to the cervicals by dint of twisting my head to catch up with old friends from the Utopian left to the far right, the ease with which Father Trennes spelled out his beliefs dismayed me. While he used any subterfuge to avoid encountering me, he recorded dozens of messages with his own sayings or gleaned from the Father's Code of Saintliness:

"Eyes on the ideal and hands in the breadbasket!"

"Monsignor didn't write for little women or disciples soft as putty but for men with beards, real men."

"Erect temples. Drive your nails in. Worship will be meaty and firm."

Finally, his mocking bent provoked me to pay him back in the same coin. When he disconnected his mobile, I plied him with questions that would also be those of any reader or readeress of this convoluted novel:

"What have you done with your Philippine flunkey and pink-soutaned Seminarist? Have you abandoned them on one of your transmigrations or are they exercising their apostolacy in Marbella?"

"Have you found any saint of your cloth in those parts or must you go and pray in Tangier?"

"Inform me in advance the day you hand Yeltsin the image of the Virgin of Fatima!"

The guerrilla war by fax and telephone lasted forty days at the end of which I received a surprise visit from flunky and Seminarist.

They arrived exhausted, off-color and jaded, a result, they said, of the successive transmigrations imposed by Friar Bugeo. The flunky dressed like the Cosa disciples of the sixties: grey trousers and double-breasted jacket, navy-blue tie, starched shirt collar, black shoes, following the norms of conventional elegance and style dear to Monsignor. The Seminarist sported a purplish wig which stood on end as if petrified, kohl-tinted eyelids, removable eyelashes framed her bulging eyes, like a pallid, over-the-hill, silent movie actress.

What a wretched misfortune to be born in Catholic Spain through centuries of implacable persecution! If only our mothers had shat us a thousand leagues from there, in Ottoman lands or tropical Africa! There we'd have grown free and lush, and nobody would have interfered with our lives or terrorized us with punishments and threats! How often we saw our sisters caged and on their way to the pyre! The slightest gesture or slip could betray and lead us to the Holy Office's dungeons, we had to operate furtively, we trembled in joy and terror between the legs of those offering their thing to our feverish, voracious lips, perhaps someone had spied on us and would run to denounce us, what misery awaited after our brief moments of bliss and passion? We knew we were damned and, certain our time was short, we rushed rashly to confront danger, the Archimandrite in Friar Bugeo's reincarnation protected us in the shadow of his convent, here you won't find women but men in flight from them, they nurture brotherhoods and wear skirts, those not chasing wenches in the refectory or pulling the devout in the confessional will mollycoddle you and relieve your anxieties, it's the only safe port in our desperate, iniquitous times, disguise yourselves as acolytes or monks, live among false *castrati*, simulate great devotion towards Our Lady and sing tunefully in church, I cannot offer you more than this, take extreme care, a hundred thousand eyes and ears scrutinize our acts, register every word and movement, record any the slightest sigh, neither the KGB nor the CIA have invented a thing, the Grand Inquisitor of these kingdoms protects their peace and eyes everything over, don't trust any lover or friend, under the lash of torture they could betray you, we traverse a universe of savage beasts, who doesn't devour is himself devoured.

By dint of self-debasement we took up the challenge, invoked the devil and his fleshly works, celebrated black masses and bestial conjunctions, got buggered on altars by the most brutal thugs, spat their porridge into chalices, consecrated and consumed it with the very unction of the Divine Mysteries

the wafers were our prophylactic!

the hatred and aversion of the common herd towards our species only aroused us more, spurred us on to subvert their sacrosanct principles, transformed abjection into heady delight

blood, sperm, shit, sputum, piss, covered the rich carpets in church before the vacant gaze of its Virgins and wooden saints

we invented rites and barbaric ceremonies, garlanded in flowers the shaftiest studs, proclaimed them Vicars of Christ on Earth, squeezed out the last drop of sacred liqueur from their cocks on unforgettable nights we evoked in mystic rapture while pyres were lit and we were reduced to ash

then we blessed our harsh destiny and glorious temerity, nobody will snatch from us a fury and ardor renewed with the passing of the centuries. Dead today, reborn tomorrow, gripped by the pull of a voracious whirlpool, we were, we are the Holy Queers of Jesus, ready for fray or foe, handmaidens of Our Lord of the Orbs and his Rod of Spikenard, we have suffered a thousand deaths and don't walk in dread of the claws of the one-syllable monster, we visited the depths of the Mine Shaft, let hooded executioners whip us — were they Inquisitors?, Nazi bigwigs? incubus tarted up in New York sex-shop paraphenalia? — the lashes lashed our backs, we wallowed in puddles of urine, a filthy epiphany, no room for smiles or jokes, only liturgical gravity, parameters of heightened passion, mysteries of joy and pain, raw desire for torture, you yourself saw us there, a cautious or cowardly Peeping Tom, in the days you gave classes at the nearby university, clenched in a tight scrum a prey to urgent urges, until the day you met dense, anxious silence and from staircase to staircase, tunnel to tunnel, chamber to chamber, you witnessed the spectacle of Gehenna, no longer seas of light darkness fire water snow and ice, but manacled corpse after corpse, feet fettered, collars nailed to necks, chained together, hanging from butchers' hooks, frozen forever in their ecstasy by the big black bird's menacing beak, must we really remind you?

you left us there, in that pitiless abyss, but we transmigrated and reappeared in the Archimandrite's circle of girlfriends, your hated shadow, Father Trennes.

we were the gasolines of May '68 and paraded along the boulevards with our frills and flounces from the Folies Bergère, hair aflame, we effusively embraced every extreme, radical cause, followed Genet and his Black Panthers to Chicago or Seattle, with Kurds, Berbers and Canacs we chorused revolutionary and independence slogans, rejected any attempt to normalize our movement, to insidiously clap it into ghettos, we solemnly abjured any principle or precept of sickening respectability

we are, get it straight, the Holy Queers, the Sisters of Perpetual Succor, the Daughters of Sour Grapes and Every Mix of Blood and will be until the end of time, as long as the human (or rather, the inhuman, *n'est-ce-pas?*) species lasts

I know the question you want to ask of me, the flunky imported from far-flung isles, about my drab oblate's outfit, I can read it on your impatient, trembling lips and in the malice lurking in your eyes, and I'll respond before we bid farewell and leave you on your tod with your pernickety book

a provocation, my dear Saint Juan of Barbès! in a final turn of the screw, to play out my role as a white bean in my universe of blackest beans!, I shall accompany my partner to the *bal masqué* organized by the National Orchestra in your neighborhood, and there all us gasolines will be on fire, will chant our slogan, *derrière notre cul, la plage!*, and after the fiesta, and with the express approval of the blessed Bishop of Vienna and the Cardinal of Rome who, according to *Millenari*, made a perpetual vow of homosexuality, we shall celebrate a rowdy sit-in opposite the Apostolic Prelature, flaunt our fans, plumes, feathers, sequins, ruffs, miniskirts, rubber tits, giant dongs, demand Monsignor's immediate canonization on the evidence of his life and writings so redolent in undeniable holiness

if you want to come too, we'll book you on the plane!

Forewarned by the layers of experience accumulated throughout the Vatican's history, the Cosa Santa bought every single seat on flights to Rome on the day set for the jamboree and both gasolines and Saint Juan of Barbès were grounded with their fancies, scurried like ants around the lounges of Orly airport.

Our Moorologist—let's call him that though the nickname irritates him—had a long wait before he received a fax from Marbella indicating the day and time set for his encounter with Father Trennes. It would take place in the Gymnasium Theatre on the boulevards: a television crew comprising Cosa members would film the face to face. He could invite anyone he wished: entrance would be free. They summoned him half an hour in advance to tie up the loose ends of the "event"—were they using the ugly word on purpose, to mortify him?—and agree the sequence of questions.

Although the chap from Barbès had jotted down half a dozen controversial issues focused on his close and execrated rival's weak points, he'd equally prepared himself definitive answers, ready to fend off cunning incursions into personal terrain or the ever-scabrous ins and outs of novelistic creation. For example: "You won't get dumb answers out of me by asking dumb questions!" Or: "Rather than setting me problems of no interest to anyone, wouldn't it be better to tell us all the secrets of Vatican saintliness *Millenari* left in the inkpot?" Or: "Recount one of your devout moments inspired by readings of Kempis in the Gare du Nord loos."

But when he got to the Gymnasium and stepped into the somber stalls, he realized Father Trennes had adopted a spectacularly agressive, disconcerting strategy. He'd stolen the light, all the light, from participants and audience: wore his hair short and immaculately combed; was dressed like a high-level executive, perhaps the director of a powerful transnational with interests in this world and the next; avoided his usual unctuous mannerisms; had been on hormones and looked rejuvenated like a CNN television evangelical.

I should have guessed all along!: he was following to the letter the advice of a much-rated, world famous P.R. man!

("The same guy's responsible for Monsignor's charismatic appearances in black Cadillacs," his mysterious neighbor in the stalls whispered. "All the Cardinals and Bishops in the Roman Curia rate him.")

Contrary to custom, Father Trennes didn't give him the once-over, didn't even try to spot him in the dark auditorium, he let a Cosa make-up artiste discreetly powder his face, answer the calls on the half dozen mobiles that rang on the table installed center-stage.

Wait a moment, please . . . Yeah . . . Oh that's lovely . . .

My credit card? . . . Just a minute!

Allô, c'est vous? Quelles sont les nouvelles du jour? Les actions ont remonté? fantastique . . .

My dear friend . . . How are things at the Ministry. You can imagine how pleased Father would be to hear you . . . We need Ministers!

Like an avaricious sponge he attracted and absorbed the light from the spotlights, leaving everyone else, Moorologist included, in the dark. Although we'd love to describe the theatre and the audience which, judging by the whispering and fidgeting, packed it out, we couldn't: impossible, but totally impossible! One could see nothing. Only Father Trennes, tribune and plebiscitarian. Already before the face-up had begun, his invisible supporters applauded him and chanted victory!

His first question fulminated like a clap of thunder—thanks to the powerful sound system—through the tenebrarium of the theatre: "Why do you who believe in nothing, my dear Saint Juan of Barbès, want to make us believe that the facts and characters you invent exist? Is this not an insoluble contradiction?"

A roaring tumult greeted his words, drowned any attempt at a reply from our hapless author.

(Besides, they'd disconnected his microphone.)

"Well, I . . ."

"I am you, but you aren't me, merely a mealy-mouthed fabler!" bellowed Father Trennes, raising his arms like a champion boxer who'd KO-ed his opponent.

It was madness. The din of the fans was deafening. Hundreds of people repeated sentences from the Book and egged him on. When the lights focused on the center of the curtain and haloed Monsignor's grandiose photo the very moment he invited the faithful to cover their ears so as to blot out the slanders of the envious and resentful like the author of this *Cock-eyed Comedy*, the hullabulloo reached the blessed in heaven. The celestial hierarchies all chimed in. As in infant comic-strips, Good triumphed. The remains of Saint Juan of Barbès poked out of a seat like a charred rocket-stick.

11 FINAL BULLETIN ON FRIAR BUGEO

Years after the apotheosis of Father Trennes—we're unsure how many due to the narrative's confused chronologies—our old acquaintance M.P., rejuvenated thanks to his thalassotherapy cures and constant use of moisturizing creams, knocked into him unexpectedly in the lobby of La Gazelle d'Or in the foothills of the Atlas.

(He'd gone to spend a weekend there with an influential presidential adviser, renowned for his flamboyance and lavish tips.)

The surprise and delight were mutual.

"What are you doing in this neck of the woods, Reverend Father?"

"May I reciprocate the question?"

"I've come to seek refuge from the world, the flesh and the devil in the Elysée's private jet, *aux frais de la princesse ou pute République*. And what about yourself? Have you given up your marketing courses and the commerce of souls? I still had you in Marbella . . ."

"Time runs on except for you, my dearie . . . As a reward for my faithful, selfless services, Mother Hen appointed me bishop *in partibus* in Partenia, a small oasis ideal for pensioners of my age."

"I can see you're also developing a taste for the exclusive locations (forgive my appalling anglicism!) recommended by the *Guide Bleu!*"

"Pure chance: I had an appointment here with a head of the Sacred Crown of Apulia, whom I tutored on the Masters. Mother Hen and the Sacred Crown enjoy excellent working relationships, do you know? Its members profess the same devotion to Our Lady and the Holy Guardian Angels . . . Will you allow me a parenthesis?"

"How could I refuse that to the confessor who watches over the health of my soul?"

"I'd like to read you a splendid saying from my recent crop aimed at those aspiring after saintliness: it comes with an extensive plenary indulgence to all who hear it and to readers of the book."

"I am all ears, Reverend Father."

(Our chameleonic hero cleared his throat and struck a seraphic pose.)

"With God's help, let us open the Broad Paths of Consolation to the juicy marrow of truth and fine, upstanding virtue. What do you reckon?"

"A very wise precept worthy of Monsignor."

They laughed together: both got the point. Wearing the habit of the White Fathers, perhaps to hide his excess weight and girth (we'd forgotten to mention that, being in such a hurry to polish off this story), Father Trennes explained to him the reasons behind his retreat into a life of contemplation after several centuries of apostolic missions.

"Considering how my work and involvement weren't what they were, I followed Our Lady of the Moll's advice: seek out peace, sleep quietly and untroubled, don't wait for the world to forsake you and dub you an obstreperous antique."

"If I remember rightly, she retired with a brawny, well-endowed lad. Perhaps you . . ."

"Don't you worry about me! I've brought along all the saints in my manuscript! Following our Founder's maxims and the rules of the Congregation for Divine Worship, I join them for canonical prayers and perform the necessary devotions. Their masculine zeal and ardor keep alive the memory of the relic glorified by Friar Bugeo!"

Although M.P. insisted on visiting the Bishop's Palace in Partenia and checking out en route the temper and brio of his saints, our fellow rejected any such out-of-hand.

"That would be the subject of another *Cock-Eyed Comedy* and the cup's already over-flowed! If you want to find out more, consult the documents I bequeathed to the Fondazione Vaticana."

Then the Elysée consultant walked in looking for her and, after a brief round of polite conversation with Father Trennes, she put an end to the novel and this pious prattle.